HOWLING OF THE UNFORTUNATE DEAD

JOHN BALTISBERGER

FOREWORD

Cursed walkers, gutter-born scum, heretical priests, and all the rest: rejoice! Herr Baltisberger brings back Dödz Bringare for another unclean romp in the bizarre and rotten world of Mörk Borg. Herr Baltisberger, in true fashion, is gloriously generous in doling out nauseating wounds and gruesome deaths. "Heroes" and villains alike get the full, twisted package. To my delight, Herr Baltisberger set the story during the (erstwhile holy) Bone Heart crusades, a Mörk Borg campaign devised and written by yours truly. Therefore, *Howling of the Unfortunate Dead* is an unholy vortex of ideas, our combined evils, thrown against Dödz and his wretched comrades. Prepare yourselves for a mailed punch to the cortex, and only then carry on reading.

—Christian Eichhorn,
Writer of *Hallowed* and other Mork Borg adventures

SCREAMS OF THE NECROPOLIS

1

THE LITTLE TAVERN in Postek was dirty. They were always dirty; it was a sign of the times, or rather, of the way people reacted to the times. Why bother sweeping when tomorrow might bring the Misery that brings upheaval, destroying all you have ever known? It was nonsensical, not that life made any sense anyway. Upheaval and tragedy were nothing to the world. The Two that were two, those damned Basilisks, did not invent pain and catastrophe; they merely sang its song the loudest.

Of course, they had help. The choir of idiots of Josilfa's church lined up to worship the heralds of the last days. You may not be able to stop the end of all things, and you may not be able to predict it, but you could at least let a man get drunk in peace.

Dödz sat at the bar staring into the distinct lack of foam in his beer. Flatter than the blade of a well-kept axe. But it still had some kick, and at the moment, that was all he cared about. He had left Kergis behind, along with the corpses of those he had served with. Just more frozen corpses to warn those foolish adventurers against testing their luck against the elements and monstrosities of that place.

He had seen companions and comrades die before— and die as badly if not worse than they had—as he hunted Lady Crol, but what bothered him was the prophecies he had heard in his dreams, whispered by a lich intent on bringing the dying world under his hand.

3

"We are given the world in icy death and burning damnation. The mistress and the master joined in the hollow place. They lead the way to a darkness unseen by all but the blind. And in that place, they open a thousand mouths to wail, drawing the full to empty, draining them of hope."

The words played over and over in his mind. Were they merely the product of his dreaming mind? Or were they something more unwholesome, something with weight? He took a sip of the acrid beer, trying to drown his own melancholy in the liquid. But between his own thoughts and the click of glasses, he could hear snippets of conversation floating across the tavern.

" . . . Ah, Josilfa and the Church will end them soon enough. They skirt around heresy too closely."

"What heresy? Don't they just yell about the Miseries?"

"Eh, no, they worship death itself. They think the dead will inherit the world or some such."

That last bit snagged Dödz's attention. He didn't turn his head or eyes towards the conversation happening at the table behind him, but he listened closely.

"Now, I don't know exactly what they believe, but I heard they don't believe He and She are divine, so you know that's trouble," the first man—his voice wet and round sounding—said. He had a put-on air of expertise that Dödz sincerely doubted he had earned.

"Wait, we're talking about the same people, right?" the second man asked, his scruffy voice earnest. He believed that the first man was learned. Fool. "The guys in masks and robes who come about and arrange the dead?"

"Indeed, we are," the first answered.

"How do you mean they don't worship the Two? I saw a group of them just east of town earlier making some sort of . . . display. Looked to be a Misery. I would guess that the Basilisks are all they worship," the second pressed.

"You would be wrong, is all I'm saying," the first said, sitting back smugly.

"Where?" Dödz asked, suddenly standing beside their table, startling the two men.

"What?" asked the first, annoyed.

"Where were these cultists?" Dödz asked again.

"Oh, east of town, along the road that heads towards the Wasts," the second answered. Then leaned forward and lowered his voice. "Is you with the Inquisition, then? Going to go and stop them from heresy they practice?" he asked, eager for juicy gossip.

But Dödz had already turned from the table and the two men, making his way out of the run-down tavern and turning towards the east.

Dödz Bringare was not a member of the Inquisition; he wasn't even a member of Josilfa's church. It was his distinct belief that the gods were dead or had fled. Anything left in this horrid, dying reality was not worth worshiping. The Basilisks were powerful, and Verhu's prophecies held as much water as anything else, but he would be damned if he believed the things were gods.

But if there was a cult, one who tapped into prophecies of Miseries that did not coincide with Verhu's mutterings, then they might have some insight into the strange dream. If they believed the world would be inherited by the dead, that would at worst make them allies of the Dead Saint Skelvik. At best, their theology would be opposed to Dödz.

Dödz was a hunter of ghuls, a slayer of the rotting damned. His bread and butter was putting to bed those things that rose from an unhallowed rest. He was decent at his chosen path too. He had managed to end plenty of undead monsters without joining their ranks, though close calls were getting closer and more deadly, seemingly by the day. Another side effect of being in the last days of a dying world.

He made his way east, winding through the small town. Everywhere around him, people were living their short, miserable lives. One could be forgiven for assuming more of the Miseries had come than had actually struck. Everywhere he looked, poverty and pestilence. Those who were in mourning in colors only—too numbed by the brutality of the world to actually shed tears any longer—went about their day, peddling wares and doing small jobs to make ends meet. The end of the world didn't mean shit for most of them; nothing did.

Dödz was worse than them; he had the most terrible of afflictions. Hope. He knew it was a false hope, like fool's gold. Worthless but for the hunger and drive it instilled in him. He knew that even if he were to find Skelvik and destroy the monstrous lich, that wouldn't stop the world from ending; it wouldn't stop anything other than one undead sorcerer's plans. But maybe it would help the world keep spinning for a few more days, hours, or minutes. Those minutes might be painful and terrifying, but they were all he had to count his life by, and he would fight for every single second of them.

He spotted the group of cultists easily. Unlike most death cults, they weren't hiding in the shadows. Dressed in black robes that covered them from head to toe and sporting metallic death masks, they worked in near silence. Taking corpses out of a nearby wagon and setting them into a tableau, tying the limbs with bits of twine to bent wire and wooden frames to create a scene. Dödz's first suspicion was that the cultists *were* undead themselves. But watching them, he banished the thought. The dead moved with either rigor-mortis-halted jerking motions or an unnatural fluidity. These men and women moved with the fatigue and weariness that was the purview of the living.

He watched them work from a distance. He wasn't alone in doing so; many of the villagers were gathered about watching the morbid display. The cultists didn't seem to mind either. It was likely the entire point of this act was to garner new followers.

As they worked, Dödz could make out the scene being constructed. A priest of some sort preaching to a choir of the dead. Amongst them, a man with teeth too big for his mouth wielding a massive sword, attacking a smaller man with nothing but a dagger in hand. Behind the priest, another corpse, a woman, stood head down, her ragged, limp hair barely hiding the smile that one of the cultists had forced her face into.

Dödz's blood ran cold. He knew this scene. He had lived it. But how could these robed figures know about it? How could they rebuild that terrible fight with Numen? Dödz certainly hadn't told anyone, and Numen was fucking dead. He took a step forward, ready to confront the cult, when the sound of a dismal horn cut through the air. The Inquisition of Josilfa had come, servants of the Two-Headed Basilisks, bullies and killers all of them. Three Inquisitors sat on their horses. They were scarred men, brutes in the black armor of their cause. They smiled at the panic their presence birthed.

The townsfolk ran back towards their houses, wanting no part in what was to come; after all, it took very little for the Inquisition to decide you were involved with a heresy. Dödz did not run. He watched, his hand near the handle of his hand axe, waiting. The cultists didn't run either; instead, they milled about, unsure of themselves, before one detached themself from the group and approached the three Inquisitors on horseback.

They spoke for a few minutes, the man on horseback staring down, his lips a grim line of zealous hate. The men that flanked him were not so stoic; they laughed at the conversation. It looked to Dödz as though they were egging each other on, mocking the cultist. The robed cultist, on the other hand, was growing more animated as they became more agitated, their arms moving through the air as though trying to explain a point to an extremely slow toddler.

This continued for a few moments more before the Inquisitor in front lifted his hand, revealing a small crossbow, and launched a bolt through the cultist's mask. The others watching screamed in horror as the three Inquisitors dismounted their horses and started forward.

Dödz was presented with a choice: let the Inquisition kill off these cultists and seek his answers somewhere else, or step in, making himself an enemy of the Church, risk his life, and then see if the cultists knew anything that could help him find and put an end to Skelvik the Profane. The latter seemed far and away the shittier of the choices. It would risk his life not only now but for the foreseeable future—what little of it there was.

But then again, this was his first lead towards anything resembling an answer, and to see that lead wash away in blood as the fanatics were killed by a different, more aggressive group of fanatics was just too frustrating a thing to watch. He stepped forward, wondering if he should take the time to attempt to broker peace, maybe end all of this without bloodshed.

He continued having this thought as he plucked the hand axe off his belt and threw it. He considered what he could say to give the Inquisitors pause in their bloody work as it tumbled end over end through the air. The sound of the weapon burying itself in the skull of the nearest Inquisitor brought his focus back to the here and now. Reality was always more bloody than ideal. The other two men hadn't noticed that their partner had been killed yet. This suited Dödz just fine as he ran to the twitching corpse of his victim and lifted the sword from his dead hands.

That movement caught the eye of the Inquisitor farthest from him, and the man began to shout. The first man, the one with the crossbow, started to turn towards

Dödz, but it was too late for him. Dödz hadn't stopped moving, and he was already there, already swinging the sword. While the Inquisitors had just clocked his presence, he had been considering how to fight them from the moment he laid eyes on them. Instead of aiming for a vital organ, Dödz sliced through the visible gap in the armor on the man's thigh. He cried out and fell to his knee, surprised by the sudden explosion of pain. Without missing a beat, Dödz drew back and launched forward, driving the length of the blade through the man's neck.

Instead of pulling the sword free, Dödz dipped and grabbed the hilt of his fresh kill's short sword and brought it up just in time to deflect the downward swing from the last Inquisitor standing. He would have preferred to kill all three men before they could get their bearings, but this one was faster on the draw than expected. Dödz rose, deflecting two more strikes. On the third, he pushed hard, knocking the other man's blade away, and raised his foot to plant a kick square on the Inquisitor's chest, sending him sprawling backwards onto his ass.

"In for a copper . . . " Dödz muttered, walking forward. Perhaps his crime would be less severe if he didn't murder all three men, but conversely, his crime wouldn't matter if none of them survived to report him.

"Back, you piece of shit. We serve the church!" the fallen holy man spat at Dödz.

"Used to," Dödz corrected.

"What?"

"You used to serve the church, and you used to be a *we*; now, you're just a *you*. The dead serve no one, and so all of that is in the past. Your future, on the other hand, well, it serves the worms."

The man raised his sword to try to ward off Dödz, but he kicked it away effortlessly before straddling the man to slit his throat. Messy work, but Dödz was used to messy. He turned, expecting to see the cultists had long since fled, but was surprised to see they were still there. Not only had they not fled, they had come closer, grabbing and dragging the newly fashioned corpses towards their cart. One of them approached him.

"Herr Bringare?" His voice was soft and muffled by the mask he wore.

"Hamfund?" Dödz asked, caught off guard to find the squire he had met in Lord Crol's dungeon here.

"Ah, yes, sir. Indeed." The short fat man reached up towards his mask, then seemed to think better of it and left it on. "I . . . am surprised to see you, sir."

"Not half so much as I am to see you, Hamfund. I had heard that your fiefdom had been the center of . . . some . . . " He trailed off.

"A Misery, sir," Hamfund supplied helpfully.

"Yes, that," Dödz said, eying the smiling metal mask that hid Hamfund's face. It looked like a shattered mirror that had been glued together in the shape of a smiling visage. "How did you survive?"

"Well, sir, I was actually away from home when the Misery occurred, visiting my mum in Grift. When I returned, well . . . " He shrugged.

"And so you joined a death cult?" Dödz asked.

"Well, I didn't realize it was a death cult, sir. They were aiding survivors and respectfully gathering the dead. It just seemed like a polite group helping out. One thing led to another, and then . . . " He gestured sort of ineffectually at the tableaux they had been building out of corpses.

Dödz looked at the scene they had constructed, the one straight from the nightmares he had been experiencing since that night in the Kergis church. "How do you build these . . . murals?"

"Oh, we're given a diagram from the Priestesses," Hamfund answered helpfully.

"And where are they?"

"Oh, they pretty much keep to themselves in Krunearils," Hamfund answered before clamping his hand over the mouth of his mask.

"The necropolis just inside the Valley?" Dödz clarified, watching the mirrored death mask of the squire.

Finally, Hamfund nodded.

"Then I suppose I'll need to pay them a visit. And, Hamfund?"

"Sir?" the dejected squire-turned-cultist asked.

"Find different friends, Hamfund."

"Sir."

Dödz turned and walked away from the scene of the slaughter and the tableaux that had been half built. His suggestion had been given for a few reasons. Death cults only ever ended one way. Death. But with the bodies of three church officials near the site of one of this cult's little displays, that death would surely come sooner rather than later. And depending on how chatty the cultists were when that happened, death would likely come for him shortly after. It wouldn't be his first time on the wrong side of the law or the church.

Worrying about that could come later. Now, it was time to steal a horse and make his way across the dying lands to Krunearils.

2

THE DYING LANDS. It wasn't a name, not a proper one; it was a title the shared collective of this world had given itself. It spoke to a fatalism so brutal and unforgiving that hope was no longer even worth entertaining. Each person, no matter if they were born a beggar or a king, knew the end was coming. They, like the lands themselves, would all die. Be it in a decade or be it tomorrow, the end had already been spoken into being, and there was no escaping that.

But perhaps it could be delayed.

That was as much hope as Dödz could hold on to. He understood the hubris of such a statement and, more so than that, the hubris of assuming that Skelvik the Profane, the dead saint who whispered in his dreams and screamed in his nightmares, was the key to postponing the end of all things. But like his life, it was all he had.

Days of hard riding brought him to the grave complex of Krunearils. It was as dismal as he remembered from last he had passed by it. It had been decades. His father had dragged him and his brothers on a hunting trip into the Valley of the Unfortunate Dead, a journey to teach his sons the family business of corpse-slaying.

A semi-successful venture. The boys had survived, but barely. It had driven his younger brother, Herschan, to seek an escape from reality through narcotic alchemical injections. He was dead within the year. Arik became cruel. Turned out he had a penchant for violence and murder and did not like to keep that constrained only to the undead. Dödz made it out, mind intact but faith in any gods frayed to the point of breaking. His mom, too, never forgave their father for the trip, for the way it ripped apart her boys, and within a month, she had absconded with a chunk of the family estate and a lover who had no interest in fighting ghuls.

All of these bitter memories flooded into Dödz's mind as he sat upon the stolen horse, glaring at the complex of tombs and graves. Back then, it hadn't been swarming with black-robed, mirror-masked cultists. He dismounted, hitching the horse to a nearby dead tree. If the horse had it in mind to run, it could easily uproot the rotten thing, but Dödz was hopeful the resistance provided by the anchor would keep the beast from running off. He patted the horse's neck twice to reassure it before walking towards the mausoleum network.

Above Dödz stretched a great arch carved into the likeness of two skeletal giants. As he grew closer, he could see those giants were actually made of thousands of carved stone skeletons. The dead making up the dead. He hoped this was artistic license and there was no conglomerate bone-fiend waiting for him inside.

"Beware the coming of the dread dawn; the sun rises again, scorching the world clean of flesh!" a voice suddenly called from within the shadows of the massive doorway.

"Beware," echoed another voice. "The devouring worms rise from rain-soaked earth, devouring, thrashing; the waters below join the waters above, and the writhing brings the end!"

"Beware, as hunter becomes hunted," a third voice cried, "and they who carry the sacrilegious blood are gutted and bled dry to feed the coming apocalypse!"

Dödz approached, gripping the hilt of his sword, taken off the corpse of the Inquisitor. It was a fine weapon, silver coated—the ostentatious bullshit would grant him a slight edge with certain monsters—but he had hoped he wouldn't have to put it to the test quite so soon. As he came closer, he saw a massive man-shaped abomination, a towering undead covered in black funerary ash. In its hands, it carried a basket, and it was from this basket that the cries and prophecies were being shouted.

Dödz frowned as the ash-blackened behemoth came closer. He could see now that the basket contained a multitude of heads, each one crying out some dire portent. The hulking brute stopped, standing at the top of the steps that led to the great doors, staring down at Dödz.

"Beware, Dödz Bringare, third of his name, last of his line, who washes away hope with mead and drowns his insecurity in the coagulated blood of the undying!"

"That is no prophecy; that is just a title," Dödz grumbled. It was true he was the third man of his family to bear the name Dödz, and it was no surprise he would be the last—he was no romantic seeking to woo and breed. He stepped closer, weary of the towering undead. Inside the basket were a half dozen or so human heads. Each one sat in a different stage of decay. All of them moved. They flexed their cheeks and tongues, using what muscles existed in their rotting faces to turn and gaze up out of the basket towards Dödz.

"No prophecy? Have we not stated enough?"

"Have you not had your fill?"

"You know the Miseries come in droves, not dribbles."

Dödz waved the warnings away, along with the flies that rose from the basket. He spared a look at the giant corpse, but it was passive, seeming uncaring at Dödz's presence.

"Still, dire warnings and stating that things are shit and will become shittier is hardly a prophecy; it's simply a statement of fact of the way things are."

One of the heads used its tongue to reposition itself and stare up at Dödz. They were dead eyes, milky and worm-eaten. It raised an eyebrow at him, somehow managing to look snarky as a decapitated head.

"So judgmental, Bringare; you are not better than us," it chided.

"More mobile," Dödz returned.

"More mobile," the head mocked. "You come to our home, to our palace. Why are you here, Bringare?"

"I thought you were a prophet; don't you know?"

"A prophet, he says!" exclaimed a head buried further in the basket. "Singular? Do we look attached? No, we are prophets!"

"Prophets. Sorry, don't you all know, then?" Dödz corrected himself.

"Yes."

"Yes."

"Of course."

"Yeah, look," the head at the top of the pile said. "We ain't got a ton of visitors other than the pilgrims, and they are horrible, just plain horrible at this. They come, and they act all worshipful. Nice at first, sure, but rubbish for interesting talking."

"I'm not here for conversation," Dödz said flatly.

"No, of course not. You're here to discover the truth, the reason for the Miseries. The source of all prophecy."

"Close enough to true. Will you stop me? Will you try?"

"Stop you?" The heads began laughing. "No. Even if we could, why would we? If you are stupid enough to seek the truth, let that be the end of you. We are not the Basilisks' misguided church; we will not deny you your own undoing."

"You're saying going inside this complex is a death sentence," Dödz stated.

"No. For some, but not for you, with your sword and your grit and the hatred in your belly. But seeking the truth is. It will unmake you as surely as any tool of death you carry."

"I suppose I will just have to take my chances with that, then," Dödz said as he stepped around and past the hulking behemoth and his basket of loose heads. "Thanks for the warning, though."

It felt strange not killing the monstrosity behind him. Letting the undead live, turning his back on them, those were easy ways to die. But they didn't seem hostile. Maybe that was the new world, the new status quo. Maybe even the dead were just trying to exist until the end came to wipe everything out. He couldn't fight every evil in the world; there was just too much. He had to choose his battles, and a few lonely, babbling heads seemed a small enough thing to let go. Without another glance back, Dödz walked through the doors of the Necropolis, ready to face the terrible truth he had been warned about.

3

ETID AND DARK. Always fetid and dark. Just once, Dödz would love to walk into a beautiful marble temple with sprawling skylights. A place where you didn't have to squint in the torchlight just to make out what was in the corners. Somewhere where the smoke from the torches didn't fill your lungs and sting your eyes to the point even the well-lit areas were obscured by your pain. No, it was always fetid and dark, with the smell of rotting feet and the ammonia-thick stench of vermin's leavings. This was the life he had chosen. And what a fucking choice it was. His brother had the right of it: drink and whore until they put you in the ground. Why bother with all this . . . what could loosely be called heroism? Where did it get you in the end? Why, it got you exactly where Dödz was: a fetid and dark necropolis surrounded by the dead and those that worshiped them.

Dödz walked over to the wall and pulled one of the guttering torches free of its fixture. Raising it high over his head, as much to get the smoke out of his eyes as to illuminate, he looked around. The antechamber he was in was a wide semicircle. Every few feet along the outer wall were doorways leading into deeper, darker, probably even more fetid hallways and chambers. But that was a secondary concern. Dödz realized he wasn't alone in the chamber. All around him were cots laden with corpses. A buffet of the dead laid out on a platter. Between the cots were masked and robed figures of cultists. They moved like scurrying ants attending to the eggs of their queen. Anointing bodies with oils, shooing off rats, writing in books, or, in more cases, inscribing sigils on the cold, dead forms at their feet. Dödz reached over and grabbed one of the attendants as they ran past.

"What?" the attendant squealed, startled and frightened. A woman, Dödz assumed by the tenor of her voice.

"What are you doing?" he growled at her.

"I'm . . . I'm taking care of the newly arrived as the holy mother ordered!" she stammered up at him, pulling weakly at her arm in an attempt to free herself.

"Newly arrived?" he asked. "Newly arrived from where?"

"Ah, Galgenbeck, these are the dead from Galgenbeck!" she said. "Please . . . please let me go . . . "

Dödz released her with a sigh and turned his attention to the doorways. "Where do these lead?"

The masked woman tilted her head at Dödz for a moment, rubbing her arm where Dödz had grabbed her as if certain he had broken the limb. Despite the mask, she looked as if trying to decide if he was insane. Strictly speaking, the necropolis wasn't off limits to those who were not cult members, but it was . . . odd to see someone here.

Finally, she shrugged. "Deeper. They lead deeper. What you find if you go deeper isn't up to us but to the Wolkath himself. If you are worthy, he will show—"

Dödz rolled his eyes and walked away from the cultist. He had wanted information, not some bullshit scripture from the mouth of the newly indoctrinated. The worst part, in his opinion, was that her bullshit may not be bullshit. He had been alive long enough to see that the world operated on its own logic, and if there was some local god pulling the strings here, he could be fucked before he even got underway. But it wasn't worth worrying about. Instead, he chose a doorway at random and barged through, thrusting the torch out ahead of himself to guide the way.

SCREAMS OF THE NECROPOLIS

The passage extended on and on at a slight downward slant that gave the illusion of descending hundreds of miles below the earth. That didn't bother Dödz too much; he had gone underground before, explored catacombs. There had been a time when doing this sort of thing excited him. When he had wanted to be a hero, when he thought doing so would net him women and riches. When he had thought that not only could he save the world but that the world was worth saving.

That had been a lifetime ago. He could feel the weight of the little prayer book in his pocket, laden with all of those memories and regrets. Perhaps he could bury it down here with the gods-damned dead and the damned dead gods. Perhaps not, though. Perhaps he would hold on to it, call on the last few vestiges of power it had to survive another day. What else was there other than survival?

Ahead of him, the path evened out and doorways began appearing on either side of the passage. Dödz wished he had taken the time to research the necropolis. What was its actual layout? How far did it go? Good questions; any hunter of the dead worth their salt would know the answers. But Dödz was more salty than his worth and refused to turn back.

Reaching the first door, Dödz glanced in. Inside, he saw a priestess, arms raised to the darkness above her. A group of pilgrims knelt before her in quiet repose. Dödz considered interrupting. He felt no sanctity or kindness towards a death cult, especially one who worshiped at the feet of Nechrubel's herald, Wolkath. As he watched, the priestess dipped a silver ritual knife into a basin of water and then brought the blade into contact with a small bowl of glowing coals. The hiss echoed through the chamber and hallway. But the truth was he wasn't here to fuck with the cult. He was here for answers. He passed the door and kept on his way.

So far, this was easy. That made Dödz suspicious. A death-worshipping cult was not usually a group that let him waltz into their stronghold and meddle in their affairs. Usually by now, he had been beset by madmen, attacked by the undead, mocked by wizards, threatened by monsters, and all other manner of unpleasantness. If he were able to just find the head priest or priestess and get some answers, then get out without bloodying himself or his blade, he would have to consider it the most success he had ever had.

Dödz rounded a bend in the hallway and came up short. Before him, huddled in the dust and dirt, were several rotting figures hunched over the corpse of a cultist, eagerly shoving fistfuls of quivering meat into their mouths. Dödz stood silent for a second, the sputtering light of his torch washing over the gruesome scene. It wasn't surprising—you lock yourself in a necropolis, you're bound to lose a few to being eaten.

4

ÖDZ STEPPED FORWARD, drawing his blade and slashing upward in one movement, catching the nearest ghul on the chin. The blade shattered. Dödz fell back a step and reached down to grab his dirk from its home in his boot while thrusting the torch between him and the creature. He had never lost a blade to a ghul's head before. He angled his body to keep the torch and blade between himself and the creatures. Now that he was taking a moment, he could see that parts of the creatures were not rotting flesh but rusted iron. As though someone had bolted on iron prosthetics as the creatures rotted.

The only thing worse than the unquiet dead were the unquiet dead that were brought about by human hands. Dödz looked them over, keeping the ghuls at bay with the torch as he figured out how to dispatch them. In the end, these things would die (again) as any armored opponent did. He moved quickly, suddenly jamming the torch into the midsection of the ghul on the right. Dried flesh and ragged clothes caught quickly, the sticky pitch clinging to the creature and turning it into a pyre.

As the thing squealed and flailed in feral fear, Dödz turned and slashed out with the dirk, angling under the armored ribs of the next ghul. Papery flesh tore easily, but no guts spilled out. Dödz reversed his grip and brought the knife back and up, going under iron ribs, up into the chest cavity. The creature didn't seem to mind pushing itself down onto Dödz's blade, teeth snapping a breath's width from his face as inches of steel disappeared into the creature. The third monster was attempting to get past its burning compatriot to join the fray.

"Fuck you," Dödz growled as he pushed with his legs to force them both up in a small jump. He raised his blade arm as they came back down, the momentum of the small jump pushing the corpse down further onto the dirk. The blade ripped through the desiccated organs and emerged from the thing's mouth, breaking teeth as it did.

Dödz pulled his arm down and kicked the corpse off his blade, watching just long enough to make sure the light was fading from the skull's sockets. He was about to turn back to the burning ghul when he was tackled by the third, unharmed monster. His dirk went skittering across the stone floor, and its dirty claws raked Dödz's face, drawing bloody grooves across the skin. He thrust one arm between him and the monster, trying to push it off, or at least keep it from getting closer. Using his elbow against the ghul's sternum to keep it off, his other hand quested for anything he could use as a weapon to free himself.

"I'm not fucking dying in a crypt," Dödz grunted, squinting through the blood that flowed into his eyes from the scratches. He worried that his words were hollow, that despite his intentions, despite his grit and willpower, this was how he would face his end: buried under the snapping jaws of an iron-clad ghul. He writhed, trying to get free from the creature, trying to get his legs up and between them so he could kick. But it gave no quarter. Dödz was getting tired. His muscled ached with a burn that told him he wouldn't be able to hold off the monster much longer.

"Ah, you must be the visitor," a voice creased with age whispered just above the sound of the rasping undead. "Why are you here, visitor?" the voice questioned.

Dödz didn't dare look away from the monster intent on tearing out his throat. He considered ignoring the voice but decided against that.

"Your prophecies concern me," Dödz hissed. "I saw the

display you lot were putting together up in Postek. I knew the scene. It was nearly the death of me."

The voice didn't respond for a long time, and Dödz didn't have the luxury of turning to see who had spoken or if they were even still there. After several moments of tense struggle, Dödz saw a pair of boots through his periphery vision, and a dagger, held by a black-gloved hand, slammed through the side of the skull of the ghul. The thing snapped its teeth twice more, and then all animation fled it and it tumbled to the side, freeing Dödz.

Dödz stayed still, finally turning to look at his savior. The figure was clad in black robes and a metal funerary mask; male, he would guess from the larger frame and shape of their shoulders under the cloth material. It held the knife in one hand, up and ready to strike like a scorpion's tail. The other hand was offered to Dödz. He reached up and took it, using his counterbalance to push himself off the ground.

"Thank you."

The figure did not answer, retreating back to an entourage of the cultists. The one in front was the only cultist who stood out from the pack—their robes were lined in silver thread, and they appeared stooped with age.

"You are welcome. I would ask what you meant by what you said, but now I recognize you. I know you from visions whispered by Wolkath in my dreams. You are the hunter who stalks the crypts and seeks to keep the dead quiet."

"Close enough. My name is—"

"Neither I nor anyone else present here today cares what your name is. It doesn't matter. You come seeking answers. What makes you think I have any?" the woman, judging from her voice, asked.

"You spout prophecies that differ from those of Verhu," Dödz answered.

There was a gasp from the assembled cultists at his blasé and casual use of the Basilisks' name. He ignored it and continued.

"So did the lich Skelvik when I confronted him, a confrontation that was being recreated using corpses in Postek. Leads me to make some assumptions."

"You know what they say about when you assume," the woman said, sounding more like a grandmother than anything else.

"Am I wrong?" Dödz pressed.

"That depends on the assumptions. If you assume I know more about your fate, or this Skelvik, then yes. You are wrong. If your assumption is that I access prophecies hidden even from HE and SHE, well, then you would be right. But again, it depends on what you assume, what you seek, what you crave."

"The truth, and a way to stop Skelvik. To stop the dead from inheriting the earth," Dödz said as he bent over to grab his dirk from the ground. There was no telling how these fanatics would react to his statement. They were a death cult, and death cults dealt in death. Death to themselves, death to others—it was a toss-up which this would be.

"I cannot help you with that. The dead will inherit the world, there is no stopping that, but that is not what you mean. You mean you wish to stop Skelvik from raising an undead army that will destroy this world even faster; you wish to stop his prophecies from coming true before HIS do."

"What is the difference? I don't care if the dead serve Skelvik or themselves. I don't want the undead—"

"We don't mean the living dead. Or, maybe we do." The priestess shrugged. "But no matter what you do, you won't stop what is coming; however, we will not stop you from trying. You wish to see, *to know*, what to do next. Maybe we can help." She paused for a moment and then nodded. "Yes, I think we can." She took two steps to her right and opened a door that Dödz had missed before. "Enter and be enlightened."

Dödz didn't trust the priestess any more than any other

cultist. But if she had wanted him dead, all she would have had to do was wait for the ghul to tear out his throat. He watched them wearily as he approached. The cultists, for their part, gave him wide berth, taking a step back for every step he took forward. When he reached the door, he peered into the darkness beyond. He couldn't make anything out. He went and grabbed the sputtering torch he had used to kill the first ghul and pushed it through the doorway.

5

IT WAS A plain stone room, the walls stretching out of sight, seemingly impossibly tall. Each surface was adorned with carved figures being tortured. The stone relief was rife with lurid detail that caught the lamp light and made it seem as though the mural writhed in agony at the abuse being dealt out. In the center of the room, a small lip was raised from the floor.

Dödz crept forward, the torch held high. The lip he had seen from the doorway was actually the lip of a well or fountain. Stagnant water filled the air with a thick mildew stench that nearly choked Dödz. He took a look back and saw the cultists had vacated the doorway—they were either waiting out of sight or had moved on with whatever it was they were doing when they came across him. He turned back to the well and approached it. He noticed then that the carved figures were not only on the walls. Their leering pain-filled faces filled the floor. Every surface of the room was a testament to cruelty and agony.

Dödz rolled his eyes, unwilling to give in to the unnatural fear that filled his gut like ice. He knelt there, at the lip of the well, staring down into the dark waters. All he saw was the murky water choked with mold and slime. Flitting here and there, he saw mosquito larvae, but otherwise, nothing. He did not notice the rotting visage of his own reflection in the still waters.

This was a fool's errand. There was nothing for him to find, nothing for him to achieve here. He started to rise when his reflection exploded from the water, grabbed the back of his neck, and pulled him down into the water. Dödz struggled, trying to break free of the grip, but no matter how hard he struggled, he was trapped. He could feel his lungs burning, his muscles aching. He couldn't hold his breath any longer; he couldn't keep fighting it. He opened his mouth for a final cry of defiance.

And breathed deep.

Dödz was shocked by the sudden realization that he could breathe. In fact, he found that other than a weird sense of weightlessness, he didn't feel like he was submerged in water at all. He opened his eyes and found that instead of the stagnant waters of the well, he was floating above a bubbling swamp in the midst of a terrible storm. Twisted mangrove trees writhed in the wind, and the hellish landscape was illuminated in flashes of sickly-looking green lightning.

Beneath him, he saw himself, or another version of himself, lantern shield at the ready, facing down another familiar figure. Across the swamp, hurling bolts of necrotic lightning at his doppelganger, was Skelvik the Profane, the dead saint, bishop of the rotting congregation. Dödz could do nothing but watch the two figures wage a bitter war in the swamp, his own double expertly weaving in and out of reach of Skelvik's spells but unable to close the distance to attack the lich.

The waters churned with the undead damned that reached up through the still waters to join Skelvik's assault on the hunter. Dödz watched as his likeness was overwhelmed by the surging dead, as Skelvik approached, commanding the very thunder to destroy Dödz. But behind Skelvik, roaring through the gloom, two reptilian heads rose above the swamp, monstrous in size and bearing draconic visages replete with antlers and unholy sigils that floated in the air.

He did not know if they were HE or SHE, but THEY looked not at the war being fought but straight at Dödz floating in the air above the battlefield.

Believe or not. The end comes. The heathens and blasphemers, the zealots and faithful. All fall. All die. All rot away to nothing. Skelvik seeks to undo our word. He seeks to become Nechrubel's foil and usurp the true way of things.

The words tolled in Dödz's brain. He could feel the blood dripping from his ears. "And what of it!" he shouted, straining to be heard above the din of the storm and his own death. Below him, Skelvik was reaching into the other Dödz's mouth, stretching his jaw as the lich plunged shoulder deep and began ripping Dödz's organs out. "What is my path forward? How do I stop any of this?"

One of the heads of THEY move close enough for Dödz to feel its rancid breath press against his face.

You do as you do. Your path comes for you. None may waylay our will.

Dödz found himself flung back and up, the world spinning away from him in a dizzying kaleidoscope of colors, causing his head to throb. It lasted all of a few seconds before he found himself sputtering and coughing on his hands and knees beside the well he had been dragged into. He was dry as a bone. It had all been a vision. Dödz attempted to rise but swiftly fell back down, unable to catch his balance just yet.

From outside the room, he heard shouting, the clash of blades. It sounded like the Inquisition had caught up with the cultists—and with him. Dödz looked around quickly, making sure both the torch and his blade was near at hand. He may not have a fighting chance, but godsdamnit, he wouldn't go down without a fight. He rose, taking a moment to get his bearings before heading towards the door.

As he reached the doorway, an armored figure stepped around the frame and pointed its blade at Dödz. He wasted no time leaping forward and trying to swat the blade away with his dirk. The figure was quick and well trained. He let his sword fall away, offering no resistance and throwing Dödz off balance once more.

As fast as could be, the armored man landed a heavy punch into Dödz's gut, sending him sprawling across the floor. Dödz got ready for the execution, intent on meeting his end as a man.

"Hello, Dödz," a familiar voice said from beneath the helmet. It had been so long since he had heard that voice, he could barely believe it was possible.

"No . . . there's no way," Dödz muttered, pulling himself to his feet. He still held the dirk, but it seemed silly now. "No."

"That is hardly a fine way to greet your brother," Arik sneered.

"Arik." Dödz could hardly believe it. His brother. Here. And in a military uniform too. It seemed entirely ridiculous. Who would enlist Arik? Who would make him an officer? Dödz wondered if they had purposefully sent Arik to kill Dödz. Who better to kill a Bringare than another Bringare? "Here to put the nails in my coffin for Josilfa?"

"No, I'm not with the Inquisition, and finding you here is a happy coincidence. I wasn't looking for you. I mean . . . " He paused, considering his words. "I have been looking for you, but that's not why I am here."

"Then why are you here?" Dödz asked.

Arik reached up and removed his helmet. It was like looking into a mirror, except instead of the rough and disheveled face that Dödz knew he presented, Arik was well kept and sported a luxurious mustache. He was older than Dödz but had only a fraction of the pained aging that Dödz knew lined his own face. "It matters not. What does matter is that you are officially conscripted."

"What?" Dödz asked, dumbfounded by the statement.

"Time to fulfill your glorious purpose, brother. With the first Misery unleashed upon the world, it's finally time to do something about it, to strike back against the evil festering in the Valley of the Unfortunate Dead. Welcome to the Boneheart Crusade, Dödz."

THE HOWLING OF THE UNFORTUNATE DEAD

I

DÖDZ GLARED UP at the grey sky. How was it that the world was shrouded in perpetual twilight, a shroud of colorless, hateful clouds with no sun in sight, and yet it was still too bright and too hot? Or at least it was when forced to carry a rucksack of supplies on his back, marching in formation with an army he had no interest in walking in lockstep with. How the hell did he get roped into this? Dealing with cults and the undead as a hunter was one thing. One man against the darkness of the night, battling the cold hands that reached from dusty tombs—that made sense to him. This was . . . this was madness. One could not win a war against death; they could not stage a battlefield against the unquiet damned.

But that was exactly what he was doing.

Dödz turned his eyes to the man to his right. He didn't look like he had any of the concerns or worries that Dödz had. He wore an easy smile, his hair was tousled, his mustache waxed, his eyes were clear and unbothered, hell, he even looked like he had showered recently. Dödz hated him. The man, sensing Dödz's eyes on him, glanced over and flashed a smile filled with stunningly white teeth.

"What's with the sour pus, brother? I would think you would be elated."

"Whose teeth are those, Arik?" Dödz asked instead of answering. "You haven't had a full head of teeth since that Brawl in Glessigvale."

Arik's smile darkened a little—Dödz himself had

knocked a few of those teeth out during the free-for-all, and it had been the last time they had spoken on anything resembling good terms. "Doesn't matter," Arik said, swallowing the anger that simmered below the surface. "I got a good deal on them, and they are neither haunted nor cursed. Who cares if I didn't grow them so long as they allow me to eat a good roast? Hmm?"

Dödz tried to hide the way his stomach growled at the thought of an actual roast. When was the last time he had seen a full-fledged bull or cow with enough meat on its bones to make slaughter worthwhile? "Why are we doing this, Arik? What is the point? We can't kill all the undead; you know that. They will always rise again. There will always be more."

"Warhawk Adalbert has a plan, little brother; he has a goal. Let me ask you a question. What happens if the Miseries cannot be fulfilled?"

Dödz stared at his brother for a moment before turning back towards the road. "Then it isn't a prophecy. By definition, a prophecy will come to pass, or else it's just the ramblings of—"

"Careful!" His brother's warning was a whip crack. "I don't mind your casual blasphemy, I'm of a mind to agree, but we are surrounded by the faithful and the zealous. So watch your tongue. I'm not so fond of you that I'll let you get me killed." Arik looked around, making sure no one had heard their little outburst. "If a Misery cannot be fulfilled, Dödz, then maybe all of this can be stopped. Maybe the world doesn't have to end."

"You can't be so naive as to think we can stop anything, Arik, but maybe you are that egotistical. And what about this Warhawk? What makes them think they can put an end to the Miseries? What makes this whole crusade, a war in order to derail the prophecies of Verhu, not heretical?"

"We both know that a prophet is an easy thing to come by," Arik grumbled. "In every city."

"On every corner," Dödz corrected.

"On every corner, aye," Arik agreed. "And what do they all have in common?"

"They're all bullshit."

"Aye!" Arik laughed. "Almost all of them are bullshit. But not all. Adalbert and his patrons, they've been stationing Inquisitors across the lands—"

"Everyone knows that," Dödz grumbled

"I seem to remember you being a man of few words, Dödz, not an incorrigible asshole who interrupts every other syllable." Arik shot Dödz a look; Dödz did not respond. "Yes, everyone knows there are Inquisitors of the Church everywhere, Josilfa's Inquisitors, bullies and thugs that lash out at any and every perceived slight against the holy word of THEY. Everyone knows about *those* Inquisitors." Arik smiled smugly, reminding Dödz of why he hated him so much.

"Adalbert's Inquisitors are less judgmental and more . . . inquisitive. They gather information. They discover, uncover, and then they verify, Dödz. You understand? While Josilfa is looking for anyone who disagrees with her decrees, Adalbert is searching for prophets whose rambling lean true and who offer some sort of hope. Isn't that worth something?"

"Hope. No. It's worthless, Arik. But fighting the inevitable isn't, it's all we have, so I suppose I understand the why of it, for the most part. Still don't know why you're here. I haven't seen a bottle of wine or a whore all day. You seem out of your element," Dödz said.

"You wound me." Arik gasped melodramatically, placing a hand over his heart.

"Do I?"

"No, of course not. I would kill for a decent drink and a half-decent lay about now. But Adalbert recruited me directly and therefore recruited you indirectly. The house of Bringare will do its part, and we'll be rewarded for it. Imagine that, Dödz, our family name meaning something again, our status restored."

"That means precious little in the dying lands, Arik. I would rather survive to the end in obscurity than die trying to give life to the shambling corpse of our familial reputation."

"But it doesn't have to be the dying lands," Arik cried, exasperated. "That's what I am trying to explain to you. There are other prophecies, other soothsayers that speak truth. The tapestry of reality weaves itself around individuals in a thousand ways. One of these men or women, maybe they offer a way out, a way towards salvation."

"That's why you were at Krunearils," Dödz said. "You wanted to know about their prophecies and murals."

"Exactly," Arik said with a smile.

"Do you treat all of the prophets you find so gently?" Dödz asked, jerking his head towards the prisoners' wagon. It was a rickety wooden affair with iron bars attaching the top and bottom of the wagon. Wooden wheels bounced across the uneven road, jarring the three elderly women who sat miserably within the portable cell. They had been allowed to keep their robes and their death masks, but it seemed a small comfort compared to their confinement.

"Hrmm, it depends. Most are carted back to Adalbert's estate, questioned, and depending on their adherence to the faith, or lack thereof, they are released, or employed, or . . . well, Josilfa is fond of pyres. Your friends from Krunearils have the bad misfortune of being both heretics, accurate, and on our way into the final camp."

"The final camp?" Dödz repeated, getting tired of having to get all of his information from Arik. Ahead in the Valley, though, the sound of blazing fire and screams were beginning to filter through the air. Smoke rose into the sky from just ahead.

"Our last camp before the Valley turns too toxic to enter without protection. We'll get our gear together, get our marching orders, divide into squads, and then journey into the Valley. We can end the undead menace for good then."

"You're delusional, Arik," Dödz said and turned his eyes back to the horizon.

Throughout their march, they had crossed plenty of camps and little hodgepodge settlements. People who lived out here in the wilderness between places, especially so close to the Valley, were desperate. Half-dead farmers and craftsman trying to survive based solely on the beneficence and needs of those that passed by. But ahead of them was the Valley of the Unfortunate Dead—if there was an epicenter to all that was rotten and still creeping, it would be the Valley. A camp on the outskirts of the Valley, at the very mouth where the cliffs on either side would funnel the undead through, would certainly attract the worst kind of attention, and so it had. Ahead of them, Dödz could see there was a pitched battle taking place among the distant tents. It did not look like the living were winning.

"I hope it isn't the final camp, Arik, because it looks as if it were about to fall."

"Godsdamnit!" Arik hissed and turned to wave at a knight. "Go tell Adelbert the camp is under attack; we need to hurry!" he shouted at the knight as soon as he approached. Arik turned back towards the camp. "You remember how to fight, Dödz? Did you lose all your army training in the years since I've seen you? Since you've fought in any wars?"

"My war never ended, Arik," he responded, drawing his lantern shield. A buckler attached to a metal gauntlet with a blade affixed to the glove was an odd sight for most even before you saw the recess in the shield where one could affix an oil lantern.

"Still using that awkward thing?" Arik smirked.

"Still using a whip like some sort of pervert?" Dödz returned.

Arik laughed and dropped his hand to the length of leather and flexible metal wire that sat coiled on his hip. "The women love a man with a whip."

"Don't be gross," Dödz suggested. He was about to

suggest a weapon that was easier to control would be better for a battlefield, but before he could speak, a lonesome horn note sounded across the column of marching soldiers. "Charge?"

"Charge," Arik agreed and began a soft jog towards the mayhem being unleashed ahead of them.

||

THE BROTHERS CHARGED over the road that led between the two cliffs and would lead eventually to the Bergen Chrypt, the home to at least one of the monstrous so-called living gods, the Two-Headed Basilisks. This felt familiar, charging with an army into enemy territory, taking the fight to those that wanted nothing more than to kill him. He had left that life behind because it did not suit him. He was a slayer of the unquiet dead. Taking human lives, while easy—almost second nature to him—was not his purpose. He was used to trudging alone in the darkest depths of crypts and graves to confront those things that should not exist.

Now, though, he had soldiers at his back and his brother by his side. As much as he detested his kin, he knew Arik could fight well enough to keep them both alive. Or at least he could under normal circumstances. He did not know if either of them could handle an entire platoon of the undead, which they would certainly encounter within the Valley, if not sooner, straight ahead in the camp. Dödz wanted to look around at the soldiers charging with him, wanted to gauge their battle readiness, but that had to wait. It didn't matter in the end. He was already charging, already committed to the action. Now, his limited time before the battle was joined was best used assessing the carnage ahead.

Zombies, ghouls, skeletons, and more were swarming the camp. Simple undead, the dregs of what could be found

40

deeper in the Valley. It was, on one hand, a relief. These were easily dispatched, mindless creatures that would tear flesh and kill but had no ability to strategize. On the other hand, if the Warhawk's band could not rebuff these simple monsters, then what hope did they have at all?

"Something worse must be there," Arik said, shouting over the rush of boots on gravel. "Something leading these cretins."

Dödz didn't answer him, saving his breath for the battle ahead. He wasn't sure if that was better or worse, really. Some greater monster leading this group would mean that maybe Adelbert's retinue wasn't completely useless, but it also meant the Valley's undead defenses were already on high alert. But as they reached the camp, there was no time to worry about who might be leading these monsters; there was no time for anything other than the clash of steel and the hatred of the undying hosts.

The problem with the undead was that conventional attacks did not work on them. Slicing at a being with no flesh did nothing; bleeding a creature with no beating heart was less than worthless. Instead, you had to dismember them, destroy whatever piece of the creature contained the magic that held it together. Often, that was the heart or skull. But you could never be sure until you had left it in too many pieces to be a threat.

This was not a problem for Dödz. He dove into the fray, his blade extended to catch a zombie as it leapt through the air at him. The blade crashed through the rotten skull, slicing into what brain was left. The creature crumbled, and Dödz kicked the remains off his blade to whip around and parry the oncoming skeleton that reached for him with dry, bony claws. He slammed his buckler into the creature, caving its ribcage inward and knocking its skull loose before he continued to his next foe.

He whirled through the battlefield, his blade piercing eye sockets and chests to tear out hearts and organs, the buckler—unlit for now—crashing into skulls and rib cages to powder his foes. On instinct, he dropped to his knees, and the crack of his brother's weapon crashed just above him, the weighted tip of the whip crushing the flying gargoyle to a fine powder. Dödz turned and charged at his brother, who, acting on instinct as well, knelt and offered his hands as a foothold to launch Dödz into the air to tackle another of the ghastly flying creatures.

The two of them danced a ballet of destruction, long years of training and fighting side by side coming back as easily as if it had been but a day and not the decade or better it had been. But they were only two men in a sea of death. Around them, the conscripted soldiers of the Boneheart Crusade died to the undead onslaught. They struck with weapons and fought well enough that a living army might balk, but they were useless against an undead foe.

"We must find their leader," Arik growled as he tore a zombie's throat out.

"Aye," Dödz responded. "Does the Warhawk not have any useful fighters?" He leaned back, avoiding the rusted blade of a skeleton before caving in its chest with a well-placed kick. He followed through, landing with a crunch as he pulverized the thing's skull.

"I'm training as best I can." Arik hissed as an arrow grazed his arm, drawing a bright red line across his flesh.

"Not very well, it seems—"

Whatever else Dödz was going to say was cut off by a horrifying scream that filled the air. It was all the living could bear to not drop their weapons and cover their ears. But even if they had, the scream tore at their souls, their minds, their very essence.

"Banshee," Dödz said simply. He scanned the battlefield, searching for this new threat.

"That would be the leader of this little skirmish," Arik agreed.

Both brothers knew that unless they dealt with the creature, the encampment would be lost. Dödz considered abandoning it all together. This was not his fight. The sheer impossibility of the task this little crusade proposed was beyond insanity. Let Arik throw his life away for naught, Dödz would rather live. He glanced at his brother, wondering if the man would attack him if he turned heel and fled back the way they had come. Or if he would be waylaid by other crusaders marching to their deaths.

"*BRINGARE!*" The unholy howl cut through the battlefield.

"There she is." Arik smirked, turning and lifting his whip to gesture at the ghostly form speeding across the camp towards them. "I'm afraid you'll need to be a bit more specific, witch!"

The banshee—both alluring and terrifying in equal measure and appearing as a spectral nude woman wreathed in flowing funerary wrappings—ignored Arik as she sped over the fight and launched an attack against Dödz. Her hands were tipped with talons that rent through the air a mere hairsbreadth from Dödz's throat as he dodged away.

"That answer enough, Arik?" Dödz asked as he pulled his shield up.

Banshees were troublesome. Their very touch could drain the strength from a grown man, and their screams could tear the sanity from a saint. Dödz was no saint, though, and so long as he stayed away from the creature's claws, he might survive. He *did* hate ghosts. He didn't necessarily fear them; it was more the fact that they were notoriously difficult to kill without faith, and the gods had murdered any faith he once held ages ago. That and their very existence offered proof of a soul and a life after death that offered even more pain than this one.

He lashed out with his blade. The creature floated effortlessly back and away from his blade before circling above him. Dödz spun, raising his buckler, watching as it positioned and dove for him again. The creature slammed into his shield, knocking him to the ground, her claws raking against the metal, pinning his blade against his body.

Dödz struggled, his free hand scrambling across the blood-soaked dirt, seeking any sort of weapon he could find. Up close, the Banshee was even more anachronistic. She appeared to be a ravishingly beautiful woman, but juxtaposed just under the façade was a rotting monster. Her breath on his face was ice cold and smelled of lilacs over an open grave.

"Skelvik sends his dearest greetings, Bringare, his kindest hatreds, his most vicious supplications!"

"A pity I cannot return them," Dödz spat as his hand wrapped around the hilt of a fallen dagger. He brought the blade up and into the creature's neck. It howled and leapt off him, floating several yards away. Dödz rose, keeping the dagger between himself and the creature.

"Do not be so sure. He waits for you. He yearns for you. He murders for you." As she spoke, the banshee darted in and out of reach, testing Dödz's defenses, trying to get past them. He warded her off, trying to find an opening or remember the words to a prayer that could banish the foul creature.

"He sounds as though he's obsessed. It's unbecoming," Dödz said as he rebuffed another attack.

"You speak so ill of the saint, of his designs, but know you this, Dödz Bringare, he is but the majordomo of the fina—"

Whatever she was about to say was cut off with a mournful wail as Arik's whip cut through her chest, the tip of the whip dissipating the banshee. Her death scream as her body dissolved in the air pierced the minds of the mortals on the field, who could not react but to drop to their knees in pain. The undead were worse for the wear. With the destruction of their master, most crumbled and collapsed where they stood. Dödz simply stood and watched as the banshee spasmed in the air, her body unraveling in gouts of ethereal blue flames and dripping ectoplasm. Eventually, the last bits of whatever she was comprised of sparked out, and a dried husk of a human heart fell to the earth. Dödz walked to it and crushed it under his heel.

"I am sorry for whatever hurt turned you into this monster. May you find peace in oblivion," he whispered before turning his gaze towards Arik. "Holy weapon?"

"The petrified testicle of Saint Barthakus of Grift," he confirmed with a grin.

"How did you convince the cathedral to part with it?"

"What they don't know . . . "

"You couldn't have done that while she was trying to claw out my throat. You waited until she was sharing information? I would assume maleficence if I thought you were bright enough for it."

Arik laughed. "Still as paranoid as ever. I think what you mean to say, Dödz, is *thank you, brother Arik, for coming to my rescue and—*" His mouth closed into a grim line, and he snapped to attention.

Dödz followed his gaze and saw a severe-looking man approaching in full plate, a shimmering golden sword in his hand. For better or worse, his chances to abscond had vanished. Adalbert the Warhawk had arrived.

III

"**B**RINGARE!" the aged general snapped.

"You this time, I think," Dödz muttered under his breath to his brother.

"Most probably," Arik responded through clenched teeth before offering a bright smile and a deep bow. "Lord Adalbert, my lord."

"You come just in time to watch my men dying at the hands of the dead," Adalbert growled.

"Just in time to put a stop to it, lord," Arik responded easily, straightening up.

"You shouldn't *have* to put a stop to it. You were meant to train them to deal with the dead, not mew like maidens waiting for a knight to rescue them."

Dödz took the time to take in the Warhawk. He was an older man, Dödz would guess in his 50s, or maybe even early 60s. Despite his age, he was no frail thing, evident by the ease in which he moved in the bulky platemail. The scowl he wore was etched deeply into his face, as were the wrinkles he had formed through malice and a callous regard for the world around him. Dödz watched him belittle and berate his brother and decided that despite the Warhawk's misguided mission, he sort of liked the old-timer.

"—can't be helped," Arik was saying. "You've been to war, Adalbert. You know as well as I that no amount of training can replace experience. The second your soldiers got scared, they forgot what I taught. That isn't on me;

46

that's on you for not bringing in monsters for them to fight before it was a life-or-death situation."

"And I told you, Bringare, that fetching demons and undead and dragging them into our camp would only invite disaster!" The two men were nearly shouting at each other now.

"Dödz, tell Adalbert I'm right," Arik said, turning to Dödz for support.

Dödz raised an eyebrow, wondering when in their lives he had ever given Arik the idea he would back anything he said. "No," he said simply. "How many castles, nobles, and camps have we seen torn apart because some moron thought they could safely control a monster? Better the dead we see before us now than the entire annihilation of a camp that thought they were safe. There is no replacement for experience, but a captive creature would have gotten loose and slaughtered everyone, or provided no true experience at all anyway."

"Our father gave us real experience," Arik said darkly.

"Our father was a drunk and a cruel man," Dödz returned, "who took children into a graveyard to face evil incapable of sleep or mercy. He isn't to be lauded or emulated, Arik."

"You're Dödz, then, Arik's brother," Adalbert said, the scowl not leaving his grizzled features.

"That is what our mother claims," Dödz said wryly.

"At least you can fight the things," Adalbert grumbled. "Can you do a better job teaching my men to fight these things?"

"No. As much as it pains me, Arik is right about that. Training cannot replace experience. They'll have to learn with the claws at their throat. Same as any other soldier, same as any other foe."

"Follow me, both of you." Adalbert turned and began walking through the carnage of the camp. As he moved, he shouted orders for those still alive to either burn the corpses of the fallen or to go about repairing the camp's defenses. He was nothing if not efficient. Dödz could respect that.

The brothers fell in line behind him as the Warhawk led them to a large central tent that must have been acting as the man's command center. He pulled the flap open, leading them into a stuffy interior. The tent was sparse, housing only a few chairs, a small cot, a table laden with maps and charts, and a smokeless lantern suspended from a pole above the table bathing the entire tent in dim light. Next to the table stood a woman in leather armor. Her hard eyes reminded Dödz of Heldi immediately, and a knot of guilt twisted in gut. But she was not the woman returned to haunt him for her death. She looked up, pushing a curl of ginger-red hair from her eyes to regard the men with malice. On her shoulder, a large white bird with a red crest, a cockatoo, crooked its head at them in strange synchronism with its owner.

"Vaneesa!" Arik cried. "I am relieved to see you weathered the storm uninjured!"

"And I am dismayed to see you weren't devoured by wolves on your little mission, Bringare."

"Vaneesa. Arik and his brother Dödz were able to—"

"There are two of them now?" she asked. "This is getting out of hand."

"I don't disagree, but they were the ones who cut off the head of the attack. I saw their fighting firsthand," Adalbert said.

"See, even the Warhawk sings my praises, fair Vaneesa. You should be more kind." Arik grinned, leaning forward.

"I don't think Adalbert brought us here to watch your clumsy attempts to fumble your way around courtship, Arik. What is your plan, Warhawk?" Dödz interrupted the display.

"Indeed. I can see your brother is more interested in the holy work than in chasing that which he cannot have." Adalbert nodded solemnly.

"Don't mistake my meaning, Warhawk. Your crusade

is insane and doomed to failure. The world is dying and us with it. I want to complete whatever fool mission you have as quickly as I can so that I can return to my own work, my own life, however little of it there is left to live. I have little patience for the fevered dreams of zealots. I just have less for my brother's incessant preening."

The three of them—Adalbert, Vaneesa, and Arik—exchanged a look. Arik looked horrified, but the woman and Warhawk burst into laughter.

Adalbert shook his head. "Very well, Dödz, very well, you aren't here out of holy fervor, you are here out of obligation, but that's enough for me. The Valley, as you well know, is the only path to Bergen Chrypt. There has always been a terrible plague of undead here, but in recent years, since the sun fled the world, it has become . . . "

"Nightmarish?" Vaneesa suggested.

"Untenable," Adalbert corrected. "No pilgrimage is possible. Along with the influx of the undead, a miasma has filled the Valley, a choking mist that makes passage deadly. It is on us to find the source of this miasma, destroy it, and clear the Valley. That is where you come in."

"I'm not sure what tales my brother has been telling you, but I do actually require oxygen to survive," Dödz pointed out.

"We have masks for that," Vaneesa said with a slight sneer. "Believe it or not, the only reason you're here is because you have undeniable experience in combating the undead. Neither the Warhawk, any of the priesthood, the Inquisitors, myself, nor anybody holds the name Bringare in anything short of disdain. You are not legends; you are scum."

"Noted," Dödz affirmed, not looking up from the map of the Valley.

"Vaneesa's venom aside"—Adalbert sighed—"we do indeed have breathing masks. We have all the tools we need to end this campaign. Believe it or not, we have been hard at work making inroads, collecting information, dealing with the undead."

"It doesn't show," Dödz said.

"That's because you're a newcomer," Arik argued hastily. "All this area we are in now was covered in that poison; the ground choked with monsters. We took it inch by inch, and frankly, more has been taken while I was off on my errand and fetching you."

Dödz raised his eyes to regard his brother. He was a liar, a thief, a scoundrel. So was Dödz, but Arik had always been *so* gods damned self-important. It was what made them loathe each other. Dödz hated how the man thought of himself as the best thing to ever be birthed, the strongest, fastest, smartest, and most charming man in existence, and Arik hated that Dödz didn't see him the same way.

"So why do you need me?" he asked.

"Initially, I was going to have you lead a second team. Arik and his team, you and yours, we could clear out the valley much more swiftly. We could find our way through and create a path to the Bergen Chrypt. But with new intel and dangers comes new missions," Adalbert said. He leaned over the table and jammed his finger at a small symbol on the map.

"This is Kur."

"Kur is a myth," Dödz argued.

"Was a myth," Vaneesa corrected.

"Kur, as you are aware from the myths, I'm sure, is a city of idle undead. A city where they . . . act as though they are living. They trade, toil, and go about their lives as though they are any other city in these dying lands." Adalbert tapped the symbol again. "It is also where the miasma originates."

"So you wish for us to lead a force to take the city?" Dödz asked.

"No, not quite. Under Kur, there is an object, the beating heart of the Valley. The Valley itself, Dödz, is a living, or rather, an unliving thing. We strike at its heart, we end the threat."

"So an incursion into Kur, an expedition to cut out the heart," Arik said. "That sounds simple enough."

"Not so simple as I would like. The chamber of the heart is sealed. We need to attain three keys from three guardians. We are also able to clear the miasma by creating holy altars; that's why we can breathe here without the masks," Adalbert said.

"We think that's what the attack was about. If the undead destroy one of our altars, the poison fog comes crashing back in," Vaneesa interjected.

"So we need to find three keys. This sounds like a fucking quest. I'm no knight," Dödz grumbled.

"Good thing we already have two keys and a corridor of cleansed and sanctified territory straight to Kur, then," Adalbert said. "That leaves one key, and our scouts have already found it. Face it, Bringare, this is the most straightforward request you'll ever find."

"You're sorely mistaken, or underestimating how many times I've been hired to kill a specific monster in a specific place. Nothing about this is simple or straightforward. But it's your madness, and Arik has already informed me I would be executed for various crimes real and imagined if I should turn you down."

"In that, at least, he is being honest," Vaneesa said, and the light in her eyes made it clear she would love nothing more than to watch the lynching of the entire Bringare bloodline.

Dödz knew their father's failings had stained the name but wondered if this particular hatred was borne from that reputation or from Arik's foppish personality.

"So you want Arik and I, together, to head out into the Valley, teeming with monstrous killing machines, to wherever this key is, fetch it from some foul dungeon and its cruel master, and then use it to kill something underneath a mythical city of undeath?" Dödz asked. "Does that about sum it up?"

"That is the general gist of it, yes, though you won't be

alone. You'll take Vaneesa and a squad of soldiers. Behind you will march a platoon. Part of your mandate, your goal, will be to erect new altars. So you go in, you clear an area, you put up an altar, the platoon marches to your position and sets up camp. That sums it up."

"Vaneesa? I assume she's there to slit our throats if we get out of line?" Dödz asked.

"Gladly," Vaneesa interjected.

"Vaneesa and Augustus are the best scouts in my army. She's going with you to make sure you succeed," Adalbert corrected. "Now get out, help with rebuilding the camp. I'll have someone set up a tent for you both, and in the morning . . . in the morning, you'll be on your way."

IV

"**BRINGARE!**" The shout preceded Vaneesa barging into his tent. "Time to wake up, you piece of—" She stopped short, seeing Dödz was already up and strapping on the hardened leather armor he would be wearing. "I see you're an earlier riser than your brother," she said, trying to hide her surprise.

"You'll find that there is very little the two of us share in common. Other than our upbringing." He ignored her as he finished arming himself. The last piece was a strange mask made of glass, leather, and cloth. It would fit over his face and supposedly protect him from the miasma, though he wondered if the decreased peripheral vision would be any less deadly.

He wasn't a fan of any of this. He knew he didn't have a choice, and beyond that, the banshee had mentioned Skelvik. Was that damned creature here in the Valley? Was this Bone Heart that people kept talking about somehow connected to the profane dead saint? He could still hear the creature taunting him, whispering in his ear underneath the constant howling of the undead that filled the Valley like a low moan of pain. At least he had received his own tent to sleep in and store his meager possessions. Apparently, the quartermaster had seen his actions in the fight and decided that Dödz had earned that much.

"Our squad is set?" he asked Vaneesa.

She eyed him for a moment. "All business with you, isn't it?" she asked. When he didn't respond, she shrugged.

"Maybe there is hope for your polluted bloodline after all. The squad minus your brother is ready. He was still asleep, whining about the early hour. We wait for him."

"Some things, Vaneesa, not even the end of the world can change." He glanced at the bird on her shoulder. "That Augustus?" he asked.

"S'blood in your shit!" the bird screeched at him, causing Dödz to smirk.

"Adalbert said the bird is a scout too. How does it survive the miasma?"

"He," Vaneesa corrected with a glare. "He survives just fine. I had a custom mask made for him. Like a falconer mask. It hampers his effectiveness, but he can still tear the throat out of a foe with his talons, or an upstart who thinks they are more important than anyone else."

"I'll try to keep Arik in line, then," Dödz lied.

He finished strapping his lantern shield to his arm and turned to find that the woman had already left. He finished his preparations and left the tent to join Vaneesa and a few other soldiers at the gates of the camp. Behind him, a swarm of infantry fell to breaking down his tent, part of the platoon that would be following behind them, he assumed. As he walked, he passed groups of men cutting apart horses for meat, latrines in the center of the camp filled with piss and shit and stinging bugs feasting upon it. Everywhere he looked were the signs of disease and famine, a war already lost. Little differentiated the undead and those who fought against them anymore.

At the gates, he found Vaneesa, a massive crusader in platemail, a raggedy priest of some sort, and an Inquisitor of the Two-Headed Basilisk.

"Shall we?" Dödz noticed that most of the group had their masks clipped to their belts, and he followed suit. Only the Inquisitor and the crusader were already wearing theirs. He imagined it had to be painfully hot in them.

"Shouldn't we wait for Lord Arik?" the priest asked. He was a slight man, and his fingers were stained black with ink—a scribe, most likely. He trembled, though Dödz couldn't tell if it was from fear, age, or some other cause. His robes, once white cotton, Dödz assumed, were stained yellow and black from the long road. He held a staff topped with the symbol of Josilfa's church and stood next to a handcart laden with a trunk.

"The Bringares lost their lands and titles ages ago, Petyr. No need for the honorific." The feminine voice of the crusader surprised Dödz. The woman was large, judging from the armor she wore. He imagined she had probably grown up on a farm somewhere, years of manual labor crafting her into the behemoth she was now.

"No need to rub it in his face, ser. I'm sure Herr Bringare is well aware of his family's failings." Though he could barely make out the Inquisitor's face from beneath the mask they wore, Dödz would have sworn he could see the cruel smirk. He wondered if he would need to add this one to the list of Inquisitorial corpses he had left in his wake.

"You're both right," Dödz said. "I am no lord, no one's master. And as our Inquisitorial friend states, I am very well aware of my station or lack thereof. As for waiting for Arik, we could get started and allow him to catch up whenever he decides he wishes to join us."

"Not even begun and already attempting to ditch me. It's as if we're children all over again!" Arik said jovially as he walked up, still strapping on his armor. "By the gods, Dödz, have some decency and decorum, even if you have to pretend at it!" He paused. "So you've met our merry band. Have you introduced yourself yet?"

"Why bother?" Dödz asked.

"No," Petyr the priest said at the same time.

"Ah, very well, it falls on me to act as our family's only bastion of good breeding. Dödz, this is Petyr Buchardt of Wilhem's Priory; it's on him to set up altars and purify the land. You've met Vaneesa Älg, our scout. This giantess is Anamarie Montoya, holy warrior, personally trained by the

Warhawk himself. Having her with us means we're damn near invincible." Arik grinned.

Dödz frowned. He remembered Numen and Elias. They had also been huge and powerful warriors, but they had fallen easily to Skelvik's forces, and then he had to fight Numen once Skelvik had broken his mind. He hoped he wouldn't have to try his hand against Anamarie. "Charmed," he said.

"And finally, Maestre Patiik Ward of Josilfa's holy Inquisition."

"Here to ensure we don't sin while we work?" Dödz asked.

"Lord Adalbert stretches the holy church's lenience to breaking with this venture. Seeking new prophecies, trying to usurp those of the HIM—the whole thing reeks of heresy. My fellows and I are here to ensure nothing untoward is happening."

"Delightful," Dödz muttered.

"And all of you are now acquainted with the ray of fucking sunshine that is my brother. With that out of the way, this crusade won't fight itself. Let's be off."

Dödz rolled his eyes and turned to begin trudging through the gate. Once again, he was surrounded by inexperienced fools and suicidal madmen on a mission he didn't believe in for an old man who thought he was more important than the end of the world. If not for Skelvik's name on the banshee's lips, he would have slipped away in the night. But as it was, perhaps these fools would survive long enough to help him find and end the lich.

They walked in relative quiet, other than Arik's constant squawking. It had started with him trying to impress Vaneesa with stories of his exploits, but the only member of their retinue who seemed to be interested was Petyr.

Dödz figured a scribe likely just didn't have the worldly experience to know Arik was full of shit.

"Wait, the entire family had risen?" Petyr was asking.

"Cursed bloodline!" Arik confirmed. "Each had risen as they died, and instead of destroying the corpses as they died, or killing the monsters—"

"They locked them all in the crypt?" Petyr gasped.

Dödz glanced over his shoulder at the two men. He wanted to explain to Petyr that Arik was exaggerating, that only one generation had been cursed, only six bodies had risen, not the hundreds Arik was claiming. But by turning, he saw they were not alone. Creatures of formless flesh held together with barbed wire and chains crept across the earth, stalking them.

"Enemy!" Dödz shouted, pulling his hand axe from its sheath with his left hand and bringing his buckler up.

The rest of the party turned to see the encroaching gnarlies. The creatures looked like flayed hunks of flesh, all different shapes and sizes, but each looked equally repugnant. Dödz had once fought a necromantic cook who had resurrected chunks of deboned meat. These creatures of flesh and iron wire moved the same way, flopping and stretching their grotesque limbs to pull themselves along the ground.

"Really, Herr Bringare? This is the great threat?" Inquisitor Ward asked. "This gets you worked up?" The Inquisitor drew his sword and took a few steps forward to stab down into the puddle of groaning flesh. The thing writhed under his blade, and the other gnarlies began moving toward him.

"Leave Dödz alone. It's better to kill them as they come than wait to be overwhelmed," Anamarie grunted, planting her truncheon in the dirt to watch the Inquisitor as he walked around stabbing the creatures. Each died with a wail, flailing its meaty pseudopod in the air.

"Last one, Dödz. Don't worry, I've saved everyone from certain doom," mocked the Inquisitor. Without breaking eye contact, he lifted his boot and brought it down on top of the thing, which squelched around his heel and squealed.

"You're mighty indeed, Ward. Whatever would we do without you," Vaneesa sneered. Dödz was glad to know the woman despised everyone equally.

"You're enthusiasm is noted Va—" Ward stopped talking, frowning as he attempted to lift his foot. The gnarly sucked at him and held him in place. "Gods, what—" he growled before shouting in pain. "Fuck! Get this thing off me!" He tried to scramble away but only succeeded in falling over, putting himself in range of the gnarly's pseudopods, which began slamming into him repeatedly.

Dödz considered just turning and continuing along the corridor of clean air, but he doubted the others would allow him to do so. Petyr rushed forward and grabbed the Inquisitor's arms, trying to pull him free, while Anamarie circled them, trying to figure out the best angle to stab the creature without severing the Inquisitor's foot.

"You can't pay for this kind of entertainment," Arik whispered to Dödz.

Dödz didn't respond, his eye scanning the horizon, or as far as he could see through the thick miasma that formed a wall just beyond the reach of the altar ahead.

"Move your foot!" Petyr was shouting.

"Vaneesa, correct me if I'm wrong, but don't scouting parties generally try to remain . . . somewhat stealthy?" Dödz asked.

"Hmph," she scoffed in response.

Anamarie slammed her weapon through the central mass of the gnarly just as Ward pulled his foot out of his boot and away. The thing let out a keening wail that reverberated across the valley. The five of them froze, watching the wall of mist, each expecting an army of clattering undead to explode through the fog.

"See, Bringare?" Ward said, covering his embarrassment with bravado. "Not so much as a scra—"

Something from beyond the cover of the miasma roared in answer to the death scream of the gnarly. The ground shook as something massive approached. They didn't need to wait long, as a thing as large as a barn pushed its way out of the mists. The massive lump of flesh and iron leaned back on two of its four legs, a dozen arms that circled its form writhing in the air. It opened a mouth lined with jagged teeth the size of a man's arm and roared. Between its teeth, a dozen gnarlies pulled themselves out and fell to the ground.

"Ward, fuck you," Dödz growled, readying his blade once more.

V

ÖDZ STALKED FORWARD. He trusted the others would accompany him and hold their own in combat, but for now, he had to figure out how to fight this horrible creature. He dodged around the gnarlies, both the new arrivals and the ones that Ward had stabbed—he didn't trust the dead to stay that way, not here, not in these times. As he moved forward, he saw the creature vomiting the gnarlies pause and then vomit more. This time among the effluvia were long rotten bodies dressed in the tattered remains of crusader armor.

Dödz stopped and watched as the gnarlies glommed on to the dead crusaders. If he was less experienced, he was sure he would feel terror and dread as the diseased remains of the warriors began to shudder and stand. The bones of the dead and the flesh of the gnarlies melded together in unholy union. No sense in fighting the dread things; standing in disgust would do nothing to end this atrocity.

Dödz rushed forward and slammed his shoulder into the first risen. The thing flew back but landed on its feet in a crouch and rose immediately to come at Dödz, its chipped sword swinging at his head. Dödz raised his blade to deflect the blow, grunting as the shock of impact rose up his arm. These things were faster and stronger than a skeleton had any right to be.

Dödz pushed the gnarly-crusader's blade away, slamming his buckler into the thing's skull in a vicious back hand. He followed that immediately with a kick to the pelvis, aiming to break the creature's spine. The paper-thin flesh of the crusader ripped, spilling rotten intestines over Dödz's boot. The thick sludge of decomposed feces and flesh filled the air with its stench. The creature bent backwards, its shattered spine not able to support the weight of the iron breastplate. But as Dödz watched, the gnarly wrapped around the spine and the creature straightened out, swinging its blade at Dödz again with no concern for the injuries. Dödz dodged backwards, barely avoiding the tip of the weapon. The rancid smell of the creature's innards filled his lungs, and it was all he could do to not lose his breakfast.

He stepped in and kicked again, this time aiming for the creature's knee. The thing toppled, but Dödz slipped in the slick of effluvia that had spilled out of the creature. He scrambled for purchase, knowing that in seconds, the creature would rise back up. He reached to his belt and grabbed his hand axe. Rolling on his back, he swung the weapon with all his might at the animated creature. He was rewarded by a shrill scream and the feeling of cutting through molasses as he cut deep into the gnarly. Dödz pushed himself to his knees and fell onto the dead man, swinging the axe again and again, crushing bone and slicing pieces of the gnarly off until both the skeletal remains and the pile of flesh ceased moving.

Panting, Dödz rose to survey the situation. Anamarie was fighting off three of the crusaders without much issue, but he knew she would need help. He'd seen it plenty of times—superior size and reach meant they could hold back multiple foes, until they couldn't, until they lost stamina and were overrun. Vaneesa and Arik were fighting the massive monster, and Petyr and Ward seemed to be working as a team.

Dödz took a step toward Anamaria to help even those odds when a powerful blow from behind bowled him over. Landing on his back, Dödz looked up to see another crusader, teeming with several of the gnarlies, raising its maul to crush Dödz's head.

He rolled to the left, narrowly avoiding the blow as it landed, and pushed himself off the ground, turning to face this monstrosity. "Aim for the flesh-things!" Dödz called, but he did not turn to make sure his compatriots heard or heeded him. Instead, he got in close. Dead or alive, if you were fighting a foe with a long and large two-handed weapon, stepping inside their reach made it difficult for them to attack you.

Dödz, on the other hand, held a small hatchet, so all he needed to swing was his wrist. He leaned back to give himself enough room, mindful of the way the gnarlies latched on to the dead man reached for him, and swung in against the shoulder joint of the corpse. The gnarly wrapped around its shoulder wept black blood, the slimy vitae oozing slowly down its side. The creature wailed in agony, which encouraged Dödz to strike in the same spot. The creature split apart with a gurgle, and the arm fell to the ground, carrying the maul with it, the decayed sinew unable to hold it up without the gnarly's help.

Dödz stepped back, now free from worrying about the weapon, and raised the blade attached to his buckler to puncture the gnarly wrapped around the thing's skull. He encountered little resistance as his blade sliced through the gnarly and punched through the rotten skull beneath. The amalgamated beings cried out as they fell and died. He looked around for his next target and heard another wail of despair, this one decidedly human.

Dödz turned in time to see the priest, Buchardt, flailing wildly as several gnarlies engulfed his legs. Ward was trying to fight them off, cursing and shouting for help. But the most concerning thing was the massive monster. Arik and Vaneesa hadn't made a dent in the thing, and it trombled towards the waylaid priest.

"Godsdamned priest," Dödz whispered as he raced across the battlefield towards the scene, already knowing he wouldn't make it in time. Indeed, despite the attacks by Arik and Vaneesa, the giant mass of grey flesh and iron teeth was moving with surprising speed across the ground, spurred on by the hollow calls of the gnarlies.

As the lumbering giant reached Buchardt, it reached down with several of its wriggling limbs and yanked the priest off his feet, dragging the gnarlies with him, and tossed the entire mess of writhing flesh into its mouth. Ward was shouting some rubbish about the vengeance of THEM and how THEY would not sit idly by as their priest was harmed. Dödz wondered if the Inquisitor knew how full of bullshit he was. What gods there had been were long dead and rotting in the grey clouds.

Dödz saw what he wanted on the Inquisitor's belt and grabbed for it as he ran up to the man.

"What are you doing?" Ward screeched as he felt the tug and rip, but Dödz didn't answer as he turned and lobbed the item into the creature's mouth.

"If you're still alive, priest, if you're still whole, use that!" he called.

The Inquisitor looked down, searching his waist. When he realized what Dödz had done, he looked up, panicked. "Are you mad? He won't survive—"

"And his chances are so good without it?" Dödz spat back. "At least this way, he can do—"

Dödz was interrupted by a loud explosion from within the giant monster, the force of which threw them all off their feet. Dödz felt an intense sharp pain in his leg, a fire that raced up from his calf to his chest. Shouting in pain, he reached down to feel the wound and found a long piece of iron embedded in his leg. He rolled onto his back cursing, bringing his knee to his chest. Around him, the others were rising.

The giant had fallen over, a massive blackened hole blasted out of its maw. From the smoldering remains, a shadow rose and limped forward. Buchardt, or at least what was left of him, shambled forward, his hand held up in the sign of the Basilisks. As he came closer, Dödz could see that he was not undead, though he probably should be. His clothes were charred, and his skin still bubbled and popped as he moved, presenting a nightmarish figure still cooking in the alchemical fire bomb he had unleashed at point blank. He turned his face towards Dödz. His lips were blackened, and his eyes had melted in his skull, leaving rivulets of cooked fluid across his face.

"THEY protect," he warbled, his speech slurred as he came closer. "Herr Bringare, you are injured . . . "

"You should see yourself," Dödz growled through gritted teeth.

Arik knelt next to Dödz. "Shit . . . "

"I don't think my injury is the main concern here, brother."

Arik looked up and gestured to Vaneesa and Anamarie, who were fretting over the mutilated priest. "It's my main concern," he said, glancing into Dödz's eyes. "Don't get the wrong idea, you being in pain is delightful, but you're my best chance at surviving this crusade. I'll be damned if you die off before we fight anything worse than a walking jail cell."

Dödz didn't answer as Arik examined his leg.

"This is going to hurt like a godsdamned bitch." Arik placed a hand on the iron tooth and his other hand on Dödz's thigh. "How did you know that Ward would have that explosive?"

"I've . . . encountered Inquisitors before. They have a standard—FUCKING HELLS!" Dödz roared as Arik wrenched the iron out of his leg mid-sentence. "You sack of shit dog-fucking scum! Warn me!"

"If I warned you, it would have hurt more," Arik said, ignoring the insults. "You're welcome, you ungrateful asshole." He grinned as he tossed the metal aside and began rooting through his bag for a bandage.

"Allow me." Buchardt knelt next to them. Dödz had been so focused on the pain he hadn't noticed the priest approach.

"Save your healing for yourself, priest. You are in more dire need of it," Arik suggested.

Dödz nodded his agreement.

"I'm fine. I feel no pain," Petyr argued.

"That would be shock," Dödz said.

"The Basilisks protect me, Dödz. Besides, my blessings do not focus on the self." Petyr smiled, the charred skin around his mouth cracking and oozing blood. He reached into a satchel at his side and a lifted a scroll-case.

Dödz's frown deepened. The last time he had watched someone use a scroll . . .

"We can wrap it and be fine, Petyr, no need to beseech the powers that be," Dödz suggested.

"Don't be stupid, Dödz," Arik snapped. "We're going into war against the dead and damned. You being slow will kill us all. You being whole could tip the balance of our mission. Besides, Petyr says he's fine. He's standing, and you're not. Let him work."

Dödz glared at Arik but nodded and sighed, turning his gaze to the sky. The others crowded around. It wasn't often you got to see someone use a piece of magic like this. *Fools*, he thought. If it were him, he would be putting some distance between himself and the scroll. Even "clean" scrolls—things untainted by unfathomable filth and darkness—were *wrong*. It thrummed with an unnatural energy that whispered promises and prophecies in indecipherable gibbering just under the sound of the blood pounding in his ears.

Petyr began to read—though Dödz would not be able to guess how he could without eyes—reciting the words carefully and reverently, as one would expect reading a piece of holy scripture. A golden-green light poured from the scroll, the sigils and runes inscribed on the vellum floating into the air to swirl around Dödz. As Petyr continued to chant, the light grew stronger and the sky above streaked with silent violet lightning. Dödz assumed it was the power being leeched from some decaying deity.

The pain in his leg was subsiding, the skin knitting itself closed, though it was hard to see under the blood that had coated his thigh. Dödz heard Anamarie gasp and had to fight to not roll his eyes. They were in a cursed valley filled with the undead; magic was no new, strange thing, though perhaps magic that didn't result in horrific things was a bit more rare.

As Petyr finished his recitations, he smiled beatifically—it was horrific to behold. "You should be healed in body and soul now, my friend. Praise the Basilisks that we may continue our journey!"

VI

"CONTINUE?" VANEESA GAPED. "Petyr, we should head back to camp, get you medical attention."

"She's right, Petyr, you're purpose is to—" Ward started.

"My purpose," Petyr interrupted, "is to follow the will of the Basilisks in ending this scourge. THEY would not have spared me from the fire and the damned so that I could lick my wounds! THEY have glorious purpose for me. Don't you understand! We, all of us, are blessed. My survival proves beyond any doubt that we are performing a holy deed in this mission. No. We do not turn back now, though your concern is touching, Vaneesa. But I will not be the cause of our failure when the THEY THEMselves have paved the way for our continuance."

Ward, Dödz, Arik, Anamarie, and Vaneesa exchanged looks. On one hand, no one was *really* comfortable taking direction from zealots; their plans tended to end in mass sacrifice for the greater good. On the other hand, if he insisted on continuing, what choice did they have?

"Very well," Arik finally said, making the decision for all of them. "If you are sure you can continue, Petyr, we'll continue. But remember your duties as our priest are paramount. If you fail in your role, we fail altogether."

Dödz rubbed his hand over the place he had been wounded and pushed himself off the ground. He didn't trust magic. He didn't like the thought that something unnatural had taken a hold of his flesh, liked even less that the priest had insinuated that it had touched his soul as well. But what was done was done; there was no point in focusing on it, or on Petyr's disfigurement.

There was an awkward silence, each member of the group trying not to stare at Petyr's ruined features, instead trying to take stock of the battlefield, ensure the rest of the gnarlies had died and there were no more nasty surprises about to charge out of the mist.

Finally, Dödz cleared his throat. "We're at the edge of the cleansed air. I assume you know where we are, then?" He directed the question to Vaneesa, who nodded.

"We should just be an hour or so march from the entrance," she confirmed.

"Entrance?" Anamarie asked. "What entrance?"

"The Mohr Krypt," Arik said, and Vaneesa nodded her agreement. "Our sources say that what we are looking for is there."

"Your sources?" Dödz asked as he pulled his gas mask off his belt and slipped it over his head, checking the straps to ensure it was tight. The others began doing the same, other than Ward and Anamarie, who had started the journey masked. Just as he had feared, his vision in the mask was severely limited.

"Prophecy."

"Gods," Dödz snarled. "Seriously? We're on a mad goblin chase based on the ramblings of a madman?"

"Careful," Ward said, his voice dripping with disdainful venom.

"Dödz, I wouldn't be doing this if he wasn't a vetted seer," Arik argued.

"And what exactly did this vaunted seer say? How do you know it's what you're looking for?" Dödz asked.

"He said that the, ah . . . " Arik paused, trying to remember.

"He said," Petyr cut in, "that the sleepers seven would guide our way in a place where heaven's hate rained down.

That within the bowels of the seven's grave, we would find those that never frown. The seven are three, the three are one, but one offers a gift that unlocks the heart of death. Of seven below and seven aboard, the youngest of the pair would face all and by all be faced before eternity became fleeting and was erased."

Petyr paused, suddenly aware that his five companions were staring at him. "Prophecy is important." He shrugged. "It's a lesser prophecy, but what else do we have to go by in the dying lands but the words of those who see beyond it?"

"Ideally, proof," Dödz said.

"We have proof, Bringare, and west of here, I found the entrance to Mohr Krypt. Above it, purple and red lightning crash from the clouds, scorching the ground in seven spaces, in a pattern. Does that sound pertinent to the prophecy, oh great and wise *leader?*" Vaneesa asked with a sneer in her voice as she carefully placed the strange gas mask over her cockatoo's head.

Dödz rolled his eyes at the woman's barbed question. "Unfortunately," he grunted and walked into the miasma. Behind him, the others followed.

They marched in a line, Dödz leading, followed by Vaneesa, Buchardt, Ward, Arik, and, finally, Anamarie acting as read guard. Unlike earlier, Arik was no longer filling the priest's ear with long tales of his heroics. Dödz was fine with this silent arrangement. He didn't want to know the others better. They would be dead, or he would be, soon enough to make forming lasting relationships pointless. And besides, the one member of the retinue he did know, he would rather shit a swarm of spiders than piss on a fire to save the man.

"A silver for your thoughts, brother?" Arik asked, shattering the peaceful silence.

Gods, could the man hear his thoughts? "You never had a silver you could hold on to before you spent it on ale or whores, Arik. You don't have any to spare for my input."

"By THEM, Dödz, you're such an ass. I don't expect you to be all smiles and hugs, that's not us, not our family, but this hate . . . " Arik spread his hands. "There's no reason for it."

"If our distance is a mystery to you, Arik, be glad for a mystery, some puzzle for you to spend your drunken nights on. As for me being an ass, *Arik*"—he repeated his brother's name for emphasis—"what part of what I said is untrue? Are you a sober man now? Have you repented your lustful ways? Have you ceased whoring and cheating at cards? And besides, none of that, none of that is judgment; you live your life the way you live your life. There is no heavenly reward, so why be kind, or chaste, or good? Be yourself, but don't pretend to be otherwise."

"Fuck you, Dödz. You are not a better man than I," Arik said,

"Never claimed to be, and I don't pretend at it either." Dödz paused and pointed. "We're there."

Ahead of them, lightning lit up the sky, crashing down to the earth, prismatic colors of reds, violets, blues, and greens in the jagged light that connected the firmament to the heavens. Dödz watched for a moment, struck by the strange beauty of the sight and the strange calmness of the silence that accompanied the lightning.

Just as Vaneesa had said, the lightning was striking over and over again in the seven spots. While the color of the strikes shifted with every bolt, the scorched earth before them painted a picture in terrible sigils and arcane symbols. Dödz had seen his fair share of despoiled magic, evil spells that wove themselves through the fabric of reality, corrupting everything around them. This sort of magic. In the center of the scorched pattern stood a massive stone door. Fingers of red electricity danced along its edges, and behind it appeared to be a burrow leading down into the earth.

"Mohr's Krypt, I assume," Dödz said.

"Yes. That's what the old maps say," Vaneesa agreed.

"And look!" Petyr rushed forward, heedless of the lightning and dire symbols etched in fulgurite. "On the door, seven etched marks!"

Anamarie moved forward and looked over the door. Though Dödz couldn't see her face, he could tell by the way she kept glancing towards the sigils that she was uncomfortable. "He's right," she called.

"No one assumed he was lying, Crusader," Ward snapped as he moved forward to join them.

Seeing that the three of them were unharmed, Dödz, Vaneesa, and Arik stepped up to take a closer look at the door as well.

"It's sealed . . . " Ward was saying, leaning forward to examine stone.

"There must be some way to examine it!" Vaneesa growled, pushing through them to run her fingers across the door, looking for some secret mechanism to open it. No sooner had she pressed her hand to the surface than a crack of thunder rent the air, making all six of the party jump.

"Godfucker!" Arik exclaimed, drawing a not-insignificant look from Ward and Petyr.

"Welcome, friends!" a voice called from nowhere, filling the air.

"New friends come to share in a vision of a better world!" a second voice joined.

"Friends who can and will be rewarded with prizes and secrets and gifts," a third voice boomed.

"Oh, friends, you simply must come and see all that we offer, all that we can give," the first voice said.

"But you must break the seal. Find the needle. Prick the finger. Join us."

"Needle?" Arik asked. "Finding a needle in a valley of bone and rust is going to be—"

"They probably mean this needle, Bringare," Vaneesa

said, kneeling next to the door. At about knee height was a circular indent, a long, thin needle, glinting against the backdrop of the flashes of lightning, recessed within.

"So we just prick a finger and the door will open?" Anamarie asked, but the voices did not answer. "I do not think I want to willingly open myself to whatever magic is here. It's clearly evil," she said, and Dödz had to agree. Arik nodded as well.

"Well *someone* needs to," Vaneesa said, though Dödz noticed she did not volunteer.

"THEM have mercy, I thought I was with warriors, not mewling babes," Ward snarled as he dropped to a knee and jammed his thumb into the recess. He didn't grunt or yelp as the needle pricked his finger, but after, as he drew his hand back, he stumbled, visibly weakened. He put a hand over his heart and stayed seated on the dirt, his breathing slow and heavy.

"You okay, Ward?" Arik asked, but no one was paying attention.

As soon as Ward had pricked his finger, the doors had reacted. Green lights shone from the cracks of the door, growing brighter and more intense as the door trembled. Corpulent flies crawled from the cracks and flew into the air, where they were fried by the constant lightning filling the air with ozone. Somewhere in the distance, voices chanted the names of long-dead things, hidden just under the rumble of the door opening. Before them stretched a yawning hallway leading down into the darkened abyss.

Wordlessly, Dödz retrieved a flint and tinder from his pack and lit the lantern in his buckler. The others watched as he took the first few steps down past the door. When he didn't immediately keel over dead, they followed, the six of them diving into the darkness below, armed with weapons and light but no knowledge of what challenges they would face within the Mohr Krypt.

VII

"**T**HIS IS SURPRISINGLY pleasant," Arik said as they continued their descent.

"Pleasant? Are you insane?" Vaneesa asked. "We're delving into a cursed mausoleum in a valley surrounded by the undead. That's your idea of pleasant?"

Dödz hated to admit that he agreed with Arik. Sure, Vaneesa's points were valid, but he had been in many a cursed sepulcher, and if he were to rate them, this one was rather . . . pleasant. The air was musty and dry, a damn sight better than the mold and mildew and slime of fresher tombs. And while he was sure there were monsters and the damned within, he hadn't spotted a single disease-carrying rat or poisonous spider. So . . . pleasant.

Of course, the lack of vermin could also be a bad sign. A lack of life made it more pleasant; it did not make it safer.

"Hello?" Petyr called, raising his voice.

"What are you doing, fool?" Arik hissed.

"Watch who you call fool, Bringare!" Ward snapped. "He is a blessed priest of the Church; you are a disgraced noblemen heretic."

"I just don't want him calling down every fucking ghul in this place," Arik snapped.

"The voices we heard, the ones that welcomed us . . . where are they?" Petyr asked, trying to explain himself.

"Welcome or lure?" Vaneesa asked.

"I would venture a guess . . . " Dödz said, lifting his arm to illuminate further into the hall. Before them, along the corridor, were five doors—two on the right, two on the left, and one in the distance at the very end of the path. "Behind one of these doors."

Of course, such a statement was next to worthless. Who knew where the doors led? It could be a twisting labyrinth that spanned the entirety of the valley, or the doors could open to a blank wall of dirt. There would be no telling until they opened each door, and with the vagueness of the prophecy they were working from, the key they sought could be anywhere within the krypt.

"What's the plan? The sooner we are out of this place, the better," Anamarie barked. She craned her neck, trying to look in every direction at once.

"What's wrong, Anamarie? You would prefer to be out there with the flesh puddles and constant attacks by skeletons?" Ward sniped.

"At least out there, we have room to maneuver, choices. Here, we are trapped, the walls close in on us, and there is nothing we can do about it," she grumbled.

"How should we proceed? Which door should we open?" Vaneesa asked.

"All of them," Arik answered.

"All?" Ward asked.

"All," Dödz confirmed. "We call it clearing. We move chamber by chamber, checking every door and cranny. It helps ensure we don't get ambushed by something coming from behind us. The undead are predators. Like any predatory animal, they prefer to ambush unsuspecting prey." He moved, holding his lantern buckler before him as he approached the first door on the left. There was a single groove carved into the wood and, next to that, the chiseled image of a skull and crossbones.

"Pirates?" Ward asked.

"More like to be poison," Arik answered

Dödz didn't bother responding as he placed his hand on the door and gave it a shove. It was heavy, but it swung inward, revealing a dimly lit room filled with refuse and long-ago-dry-rotted furniture. In the center of the room, Dödz could just make out six jugs sitting on the floor. He stepped in, looking towards the dark corners of the room, trying to spot any threats.

"Welcome! Welcome!" shouted a wet-sounding, high-pitched voice.

"Goblin," Arik hissed, grabbing is whip off his belt. Dödz wondered what good a weapon like that would be in close quarters.

"Goblin *king*" the voice corrected as the creature waddled into the light. Most zombies Dödz had faced were the more recent sort, rotting and putrescent. This creature had been entombed—it was desiccated, its flesh tight and dry, the rot of time rather than decomposition. It was larger than any goblin Dödz had seen before but unmistakably one of the horrid creatures. "Xilk, at your service. Here to offer you a game, a riddle, an enigma for your benefit."

"We are not here to play games," Ward snarled, his hand hovering near his sword.

"What game?" Dödz asked, ignoring Ward.

"Ah good, a smart one." Xilk smiled cruelly, the corners of his mouth cracking. "I have jugs of blood before you. All but one is mine. Taken and laid out as I was embalmed. The last comes from a saint, a saint of holy goodness. And if you drink from that, oh such dreams are yours. Drink from mine, drink from mine and you will join my kingdom as my kind." The creature folded his hands across his gaunt belly and grinned. "Choose."

"And if we choose not to play?" Arik asked.

Xilk's eyes glinted cruelly. "Not an option now you've opened the door, you heard the rules; leave and I will make sure you wake tomorrow as my cursed kin."

"Fine, this is idiotic anyway. King or not, no goblin can outsmart a man." Arik strode forward and looked over the jugs. "The jugs are numbered, your door has one mark on it, so it's the first jug." He laughed and grabbed for it.

"Wait!" Dödz called and joined Arik, looking across the six jugs. "Xilk, how many jugs are there?"

Xilk, who had smiled maniacally as Arik lifted the jug, froze. His smile faltered. "You can see how many jugs there are . . ." he stammered.

"I can see, but answer anyway. How *many* jugs are there?"

"You can *see* the jugs; you can *find* them before you," Xilk repeated, a nasty tone entering his voice.

"We can see them now, without doing anything else?" Dödz asked. He stepped closer to Xilk, looming over the smaller goblin king.

"I said you can see them," he hissed, his cloudy eyes darting towards the rotten bed.

"Mmm," Dödz agreed. "Arik, put that down and check under the thing's bed."

"You don't need to do that. You can choose the one you picked up!" Xilk shrieked.

Arik set the jug he had been holding down and walked to the bed, crouching down, grunting. "There's a jug under here . . ." he called. "Marked with a seven."

"Seven. Seven bolts of lightning, seven sleepers, seven Miseries . . ." Dödz shook his head. "What do you think, Xilk, is seven the magic number?"

The goblin king's teeth were bared in a jagged, angry snarl. He locked eyes with Dödz, and for a moment, Dödz thought the creature would attack him. "Who knows?" he growled instead.

"Go ahead, Arik," Dödz called back.

Without turning, he could hear the sound of Arik guzzling, and then: "Haha! By THEM! Gold!"

Dödz turned to see that Arik, his chin covered in thick red blood from drinking, had found a solid gold charm in the shape of a human heart within the jug. He turned back around to find Xilk creeping back into the shadows, grumbling, "The next to come will choose better." He crouched in the darkness of the corner, curling into a ball.

Dödz watched him for a few moments to make sure he was truly inert and then nodded. "Clean yourself up, Arik; you look like a ghul. Obviously, no key in this room." He turned and pushed his way past Anamaria and Ward to get back into the hallway.

"I just drank a pint of blood," Arik said as he joined Dödz.

"You probably could have just poured it out," Dödz pointed out.

"You told me to drink—"

"No, the goblin told you to drink. I said no such thing." He pointed across the hall to the door directly in front of them. It bore a groove just like the first door, but carved next to that was the image of a sleeping woman. "But tell you what, I'll deal with the next mystery."

"Such gentlemen," Vaneesa sneered.

"I would rather be alive than kind," Dödz answered her as he crossed the hall to push the second door open.

VIII

AS THE DOOR swung open, the light from Dödz's shield illuminated the chamber within. Unlike Xilk's room, this chamber was sparse, devoid of the debris of ruin. A thick coat of dust covered the floor, and in the center of the room, a stone platform rose from the ground. Atop the platform, the figure of a sleeping woman lay, clad in a white dress that clung to her sleeping curves and flowed over the side of her make-shift bed like waves of ivory.

Dödz walked into the room, raising his light high to banish the shadows in the corners, looking towards the ceiling for any ambushers. "All clear," he called back and approached the dais. She was breathtaking, porcelain skin, perfect complexion, and her golden hair fell around her like a shimmering golden mane. Her full lips were parted slightly as if waiting for a kiss. All in all, she was a strange sight, such lovely perfection in such a terrible place.

Dödz was not a terribly big fan of perfection. He found it off-putting, unnatural. He preferred if his dance partners had scars and experience. But he knew others would feel differently. He frowned.

"Keep Arik back," he called back.

"Keep me back from what?" Arik asked, moving beside Dödz. "By THEM! Look at her!" He stepped closer, peering down at the woman. "She's gorgeous. Wouldn't kick her out of the sack for trying, that's for sure. So peacefully sleeping too. Must be a curse."

"A curse?" Petyr asked, moving up to the dais and hissing through his teeth as he laid eyes on the sleeping beauty.

"Have you never seen a woman before?" Vaneesa asked.

"Never saw one he didn't think was his right," Dödz answered for Arik.

"Fuck you, Dödz," Arik snarled before turning back to the woman. "You know how to break a curse like this, right? A kiss from a handsome prince."

"Too bad there are no handsome men or princes about, then," Vaneesa said, the sneer obvious in her voice.

"You simply have no taste. I suspect you prefer the company of women, or of dogs," Arik said before he began to lean forward.

Dödz caught his shoulder and pulled him back.

"I find it disturbing enough that your first thought on seeing a woman is to molest her, but it's even worse when she's dead, Arik."

"Dead? What are you talking about? There's no rot, no flies . . . "

"I must admit, Herr Bringare, I have trouble believing you as well," Petyr said.

"Do you?" Vaneesa snapped. "We're in a krypt in the center of the Valley of the Unfortunate Dead, and you have trouble believing she may be dead?"

"There's also no signs of any carrion feeders, no flies, maggots, roaches, or rats. Not anywhere. She's cursed, but it is not with sleep," Dödz said, lifting his lantern above the woman's form. Now, with the light so close to her flesh, they could see how it was sunken and tight in places it should not be. Dödz used his other hand to peel her eye open, revealing the milky orb underneath.

"If you kiss her, you'll either be kissing a corpse again or—"

"Again?" Vaneesa asked.

"Shut the fuck up," Arik snapped.

"Or she'll wake and bite your face off. Either way, no skin off my lips," Dödz said with a cruel grin before turning to leave the room and try the next door. The others followed after, including a sullen and irritated Arik.

Upon opening the next door, this one decorated by one groove and the image of a drop of water, they were hit by a wall of mildew stench. Dödz frowned as he looked inside. There was a stagnant pool of water in the center of the chamber, and in that, a single skeletal arm stuck out, grasping for something in the empty air.

"What should we do?" Petyr asked as he stepped up beside Dödz.

"Look in the water, see if we can spot any sort of key there, avoid the dead." Dödz shrugged. "Of all the crypts filled with death I have been in, this has been the most peaceful by far." He threw a meaningful look to Arik—in their experience, peaceful usually meant a calm before the storm. Two more rooms after this to clear, and who knew what sort of evil existed in this place.

The group fanned out, walking along the edge of the water, searching for any sign of something within its damp embrace. Pond scum covered the surface, making it difficult to make out what lay at the bottom. While the others peered into the depths of the cistern, Dödz kept his eyes on the skeletal arm. It waved around, grasping at nothing, but did not otherwise move.

"What do you think, Herr Bringare?" Anamarie asked as she stopped next to him.

He didn't know why everyone kept asking him for his opinion. Arik was theoretically in charge of this group. Or maybe it was Ward, the Inquisitor. Or the priest, hells. Anyone other than Dödz had more reason to be considered a legitimate leader.

He shook his head. "While it's possible that the skeleton under the waves has something to do with this, I would just as soon check the other rooms first."

"Scared of a skeleton, Bringare?" Ward asked.

"Remember what happened last time you attempted to mock me about fear of the undead, Inquisitor? Look at your priest if you don't. For that's on you," Dödz said and then turned to make for the door.

"I would rather you not use me to fuel your jabs at one another," Petyr called.

"It isn't a jab, priest. It's the truth." He turned, glancing at the five of his companions. "Petyr, you're in charge of creating altars, places that drive back the miasma and make it safe for us, right?"

"Sir."

"Head out of here and set up an altar a bit away, then signal the Warhawk so that they can make camp nearby. But not too nearby. I don't want this cursed place drawing more inquisitive crusaders to their doom. Anamarie, you attend him, keep him safe out there."

"You're sending our best protection and strongest fighter out before we clear the tomb?" Arik asked incredulously.

"I feel better about our chances to survive without her than I do his, Arik." He didn't feel the need to point out the tremor of fear in Anamarie's steps. Her fear would make her more of a hindrance than a boon should a fight break out. Her claustrophobia was obvious to him, but if others did not notice, he would spare her the humiliation of owning up to it.

Petyr looked at Ward as if asking permission. Ward slowly nodded—as much as it obviously irked him to agree, he had to admit it was probably the best move. Without any argument from Anamarie, the two left the room and headed back for the entrance.

"Two more rooms," Dödz said. "Then we can join them."

The fourth door was marked with the singular groove and a crude carving of bones. Dödz looked at the others before opening the door to reveal a chamber filled with bones. Ward stepped past him into the room, wincing as a bone crunched under his foot. Immediately, a fog filled the room, a swirling cloud that seemed to form faces and moans as it moved. Ward stumbled back, directly into Arik.

"Watch it!" Arik snarled.

"Help me." A low moan filled the room. "Help me become whole!"

"What help do you need, spirit!?" Arik called into the mist.

"Make me whole!" it cried again before manifesting in the center of the chamber. "I can't find my femur!"

Dödz noticed that, in one corner of the room, someone or something had nearly finished constructing a full skeleton. It didn't look human. He could see elements of animal bones within it, crocodilian jaws, bat-like wings. He turned his attention back to the wraith. It had a generally human shape; he just didn't trust it.

"Make you whole, and what happens then?" Dödz asked.

"I'll be free. I'll reward you, I'll thank you, make your journey easier. I know the secrets of the valley. I know how you can succeed!" the spirit wailed.

"Succeed?" Ward asked. "Succeed in what?"

As Ward conversed with the thing, Vaneesa leaned over. "I think I could find the femur if I needed to. There are a lot of bones, but most of them are broken and small, or obviously skulls . . . It would take time, but . . . "

Dödz shook his head. "I don't think we need to." He put a hand on Ward's shoulder.

"It's trapped here, Inquisitor. If we release it, we're

responsible for every death it causes, every blasphemy it commits."

"No! No no no no no no no!" the thing screamed, swirling around the room and causing a vortex to form, slinging bones in a swirling tornado of calcified shards.

Dödz stepped back and pulled Ward back across the threshold of the door. No bones struck them. The creature gnashed its spectral teeth and charged but smashed against an invisible barrier at the door, dissipating for a moment before reforming once more in the center of the room.

"This is less a crypt and more of a prison," Dödz said.

"Each room is a cell, and each prisoner kept by a riddle. They want us to solve the puzzles and free them," Arik mused.

"It's why we were welcomed in," Dödz agreed.

"And why there are no vermin or other dangers." Vaneesa gasped. "What would happen if we freed any of these . . . things?"

"Nothing good. At best, they would kill us and await the next idiots, and worst, they would kill us and then head out into the valley to perpetuate greater evil than we could imagine," Dödz said.

"Then we should kill each of them! End the threat once and for all," Ward said resolutely.

"Or, hear me out," Arik said. "We get what we came for and get the fuck out. Some of these creatures require very specialized means of dispersal, and we would be putting ourselves at great danger in facing them. Better to get what we need, leave, and then seal the entrance."

Ward looked between the brothers, hoping Dödz would argue with Arik. But as much as Dödz detested his brother, they had both spent their lives hunting damned things that would not stay dead. He was a fop and an ass, but he was no fool when it came to these things.

Dödz reached out and closed the door, trapping the wraith within. "One more chamber, one more chance." He stepped back and headed for the final door at the end of the hallway. This one was marked by three deep grooves. There was no carving next to it, no obscure hint of what they might find. Dödz glanced Arik, Ward, and Vaneesa before placing a hand on the door and shoving it open.

Violet light spilled out of the room, and they heard a voice, the same voice that had greeted them when they entered the krypt.

"Welcome, welcome. Finally, you come to us. I knew you would make it. I knew you would survive the trials set before you. Now, come and bask in the glory and favor of the entropic trinity!"

The four entered the chamber. Unlike the prior rooms, the chamber seemed more decorated, or maybe it was simply better lit by the sickly violet light that seemed to swirl around the room like a living thing. The room was shaped like a funnel, a long hallway leading to a triangle chamber. In each corner of the chamber sat a throne carved into the stone, grand things covered in filigree relief. In each throne sat a corpse with glowing purple eyes that watched the party as they entered. The corpses, dressed in grey and black ragged robes, were chained by their wrists and ankles, the chains themselves leading up into the darkness of the ceiling somewhere too far above them to be natural.

"Hello, mortals, and welcome to our home."

IX

ÖDZ LOOKED AROUND, taking the time to examine each figure as Arik and Vaneesa joined him. Ward stayed near the entrance to the door, looking like he was ready to bolt at a moment's notice.

"Oh, tell your friend they need not cower; we mean you no harm," the voice of a lich croaked out.

"No harm more than has already been done," said the next.

"No harm at all. We offer such things as will reward you for dutiful service," the third intoned.

"He's fine where he is," Dödz replied. "And who are you? Other than the entropic trinity, or whatever you call yourselves, who are you really?"

There was silence for a moment. Things like this—things used to sparking awe in mortals—tended to get thrown off when you didn't show proper fear, but it gave them only two options: continue the charade of kindness or throw it off and attack. Dödz would rather get to the conclusion of this little act as quickly as possible.

"Karn, the Marrow Whisperer," one announced.

"Nordorotz, high king of the rot!" the second cried.

"Visdomstand," the third said.

"No lofty title for you?" Arik asked Visdomstand.

"None needed," the lich replied.

"Does knowing their names help you at all?" Vaneesa asked Dödz.

"No, but it makes it easier to address them." Dödz

87

shrugged. "Every other room here has offered some sort of puzzle, some entity within seeking to be free of this prison. What about you three? Are you asking us to free you?"

"No," Nordorotz said.

"Yes!" cried Karn.

"No," whispered Visdomstand.

"Two no's and a yes. I would assume the trinity would act as one," Arik suggested.

"We need not be together to be one," Nordorotz said with a sniff.

"So freeing one of you is tantamount to freeing all of you. But I'm not seeing the puzzle, or the object we are looking for," Vaneesa said. "We should go. Obviously, they have nothing for us."

"WAIT!" all three shouted at once, causing the entire krypt to shake.

"We have what you want," Visdomstand hissed.

"We each ask something," Nordorotz whispered.

"We each offer something," Karn said, straining at his restraints.

Arik heaved a great sigh and shrugged. "You know, it's only ever groups of evil things that do this chorus bullshit."

Dödz nodded. "They think it makes them mysterious and otherworldly."

"But it just makes them look like assholes," Vaneesa finished.

"See?" Dödz asked. "We can do that too. Let's cut to the chase. What do you have, and what are you asking?"

If the trinity was put off by the mortals mocking them, their rictus grins didn't betray their ire. "For my freedom, I offer a prize," Karn said through gritted teeth.

"For a sacrifice, I offer a gift," Nordorotz said.

"And you?" Dödz asked.

"For a payment, I offer a secret," Visdomstand groaned.

"A prize, a gift, and a secret," Arik repeated. "I mean, it's obvious that the prize is the key, right? Let's cut these chains and be through."

"Cut his chains?" Vaneesa asked. "So he can join the undead legions in cutting us down? He didn't say they would let us live if we freed him. What good is a prize for your corpse?"

"He's wrong anyway," Dödz said, staring straight at Nordorotz. "Isn't he?"

"Free him and find out," Nordorotz said through his death-grin, the violet light from his eyes growing bright.

"No. I think not. The prophecy said a gift would unlock the heart. It's you," Dödz accused. Behind him, Vaneesa and Arik turned away from Karn to flank Dödz. "So a sacrifice—what is it you want sacrificed?"

"Nothing you can't live without, nothing you haven't lived without. Above us, coming closer, an army of life marching to their death. I ask only that you hasten ten of those lives towards the end, towards me, into my embrace. Bring me ten Crusaders, and I will give you my gift." Despite the fact that the creature's face had not moved, his dead smile seemed to stretch, becoming impossibly broad in his decayed skull.

"We're not killing Crusaders for this piece of shit," Vaneesa growled.

"Ten lives is not that steep a price to pay for—" Arik started, but before he could finish, Vaneesa had pulled a short sword and pressed it to his throat.

"Speak; finish your thought," she growled.

Dödz rolled his eyes behind his gas mask. "I have another idea." He lunged forward, bringing his bladed fist around in a savage arc towards the creature's skull. One finger of its chained hand twitched, and Dödz froze in mid lunge, frozen in the air, his blade a few scant inches from the lich's head.

"Oh, my poor deluded fool, how wrong you are, how foolish. I would have given you that which you sought. All it would have cost you is ten strangers. Now. Now you all die, you all die, and the next visitor will be less foolish, less stubborn. Understand that, mortal. Your disobedience and courage amount to nothing. Your sacrifice will be nothing but new bones in the wraith's room to scatter in his rage."

"You fucking monsters!" Vaneesa roared. "Release us! I promise the full wrath of the Warhawk will come and end—"

"And die," Karn finished for her. "You will all die."

Nordorotz lifted one hand off his throne, violet light crackling across the bony claws. He reached one finger out and touched Dödz, sending a current of excruciating pain through him. Dödz screamed, his body frozen, suspended in the air.

"Death can be painless," Nordorotz whispered.

"A release from the world," Karn agreed.

"But it does not have to be; it can be beautifully torturous," Visdomstand chortled.

"But no matter what it is, yours comes now." Nordorotz sighed and pushed more power into Dödz.

Dödz felt his skin crackling. Any moment now, it would blister and flake, his eyes would melt, his bones would— the pain stopped. He floated there, panting, all three liches silent and still.

"Master," Karn said.

"Master cannot mean this," Visdomstand growled.

"You ask too much. It cannot be this one!" cried Nordorotz. As one, the liches tilted their heads, listening to some unheard response. As they sat in stony silence, their glowing eyes dimmed and brightened in tandem, moving through the color spectrum from violet to blue to green to red, and finally, their eyes brightened and returned to their violet hue. "You are a strange paradox in this play, Dödz Bringare."

The lich lowered his arm and, with a gesture from one finger, used Dödz as a puppet, dragging his arm down so that instead of the blow he had been caught mid-swing in landing on the lich's skull, it was aimed at his midsection. "I look forward to watching it unfold."

Suddenly, Dödz was unstuck. He would have expected

to simply fall, but instead, his attack carried through as though he had never been halted. The blade tore through Nordorotz's stomach, spilling rotting intestines crawling with roaches onto the ground. The creatures screamed with tiny human faces, scuttling as quickly as they could back up the intestinal lining, back into the lich's body. There, nestled in the putrescent ropes, glittered a filthy ivory key.

Ward stepped forward and grabbed the key. "Now what happens?"

"You will let them escape?" Karn roared, his eyes blazing bright.

"We are ordered—" Nordorotz shouted back.

"You were ordered. We desire our freedom!" Visdomstand added his voice to the cacophony.

"Now, we run," Dödz suggested.

No one argued, and they beat a hasty retreat as the liches began slinging spells at one another, seeming to be oblivious to the mortals fleeing their tantrum. They didn't stop until they pushed through the doorway back into the valley. Outside, they were greeted by clear air, the miasma having been banished. In the distance, they could see the banners of the Crusaders as they marched toward whatever camp Anamarie and Petyr had set up. As soon as they were out, Dödz stumbled and fell to one knee. The pain the lich had put him through made his muscles burn; every inch of him felt sore and abused.

"Are you okay?" Vaneesa asked Dödz as she reached up to remove her mask.

"He's fine," Arik snapped, whipping off his own mask. "We got the key, we survived, no one died. That's a successful delve if ever I've seen one. Come, let's join the others and make camp." He marched off in the direction of the Crusaders.

Vaneesa glowered at Arik taking charge, spared a last look at Dödz, then followed suit.

"No love lost between you two, is there?" Ward asked, offering Dödz a hand up.

"Very astute," Dödz agreed as he took the hand and let himself be pulled up. "But he isn't wrong. A bit of pain is a small price to pay. We were lucky."

"Lucky? Or is there some reason the creatures were ordered to give you the key?" Ward asked. He kept his voice casual and neutral, but Dödz could hear the implicit accusation and threat.

"Not that I know of," Dödz answered as he began undoing the ties of his mask. "But I have earned the attention of more than one monstrosity in this lifetime. I promise, though, Inquisitor, in this at least, we are allies. I want nothing more than to see them all embrace a final death."

Ward stared at him for a moment and then nodded. "I may be a fool, but I think you're probably an honest piece of shit; at least you have that going for you." He turned and headed off himself. Dödz watched him for a moment and then sighed and followed.

By the time Dödz reached Petyr and Anamarie, the Crusaders had already arrived and begun setting up a camp. Dödz watched as his brother and Vaneesa argued with each other before the Warhawk, Petyr, and Ward headed for a clump of priests and holy men, likely to give their own reports. Anamarie, for her part, was doing actual work, warning crusaders to stay away from the flashing lights in the distance, knowing if any of them descended into Mohr Krypt, it would be their deaths.

Within all of this, Dödz found the company mess and grabbed a few rations before pushing through the camp to find his tent. He didn't care to socialize or to chase glory. He just wanted to eat, set up his tent, and rest before the next step in this nightmare played out. A good rule for any hunter—hell, any soldier—rest when you could. Fighting in exhaustion was almost as bad as fighting injured or drunk.

It took some doing, and by the time he found his tent, he had finished eating his meager share. He didn't mind, though. He set up his tent quickly and headed inside, praying he would be able to get a good night's rest before whatever new hell awaited him tomorrow. He was about to douse his lantern when the entrance to his tent rustled and Vaneesa slipped in with Augustus on her shoulder, a bundle of bedding and gear in her arms.

He frowned. "What are you doing here?"

"I . . . " She snapped the first word, her anger bleeding through the single syllable, before she swallowed and softened her tone. "I would like to sleep here, in your tent."

"You don't have your own tent?" Dödz asked.

"I do," she replied, still standing in the door of his tent, looking awkward and uncomfortable. "There are a group of . . . *men* near my tent. They leer. They think I don't see them, hear them. They talk about how they can . . . fix my attitude, how they'll—"

Dödz lifted a hand, cutting her off. "I get the picture. You can sleep here." He stepped up to her and took her bedding from her, tossing it down on the opposite side of the tent to his. "But why here? I would think staying in the command tent, nearer to Adalbert, would be your preference. You've made your distaste for all Bringares plain enough."

"Yes. You and your brother are scum," she said as she began setting down her gear, Augustus flapping his wings to get balanced before flying to the ground to look for insects to eat. "But I don't think you're the type of scum to force yourself on someone. I think you're the sort of scum that has given up and sees the worst in everyone. You're the sort of shit-fucker who gives nothing and thinks so long as you take nothing, you're doing the world a favor. So, you're safe. For me, anyway." She looked back up at him. "Am I wrong?"

"Not in the least," Dödz admitted. "But tell Augustus if he shits on my stuff or wakes me, I'll be having chicken for breakfast."

"Fuckwit can try!" Augustus squawked.

Dödz was forced to smile as he doused the lamp and lay down on his own bedding. He would be loath to admit it, but he was growing fond of the feathered menace.

WHEN DÖDZ WOKE, he found that Vaneesa and Augustus were already gone, though her bedding and bits of gear remained. He rose and dressed quickly before heading out. The camp was already coming to life. He considered heading to the mess, but he could see that whatever they were butchering for meat didn't look like a healthy animal. He wasn't above eating dog, no one in this age was, but a feral hound that made the Valley of Unfortunate Dead its home was not a thing that Dödz wanted to put in his mouth. He wasn't that desperate yet. Besides, the sickly sweet smell of gangrenous flesh wafting from the medic's tent was putting him off his appetite anyway.

Instead, he made his way towards the command tent to speak with Adalbert and discover what the next leg of this fiasco was. He was halfway to the tent when a group of five men surrounded him.

"You're that Bringare guy's brother, ain't you?" asked a crusader with too few teeth in his skull.

"That depends on why you're asking," Dödz said, looking around the crowd that circled him. Rough-looking men, half-starved. He could see tattoos peeking out of their sleeves, matching, likely some sort of gang or cult affiliation, though not one he was familiar with.

"You know it's funny," the man said, and Dödz figured he must be their leader. Maybe he had the most teeth or was just the largest of them. He had a bit more armor than the others, but really, the one doing the talking was usually the leader when you were dealing with scum like this. Hardly ever the strong silent types. "Yer brother was trying real hard to get with Lady Vaneesa. Didn't seem to get too far, though."

"Mm," Dödz responded. He could see where this was going. The only question was how far would they take it.

"You, on the other hand, you go on one little outing, and look who is spending her time in your tent. Seems like you got the magic touch." The man's voice had more than a little gravel to it.

Dödz wondered if it were natural or if he were trying to make himself sound more intimidating. Either way, he had no interest in engaging. He walked forward with the intention of pushing past the men.

"We ain't done here, boy," the leader snarled, brandishing a dirk. "I lay claimed to that woman. Everyone knows it."

"Apparently not her," Dödz replied. The man's face turned red. He could, of course, explain that nothing had happened and that Vaneesa disliked him as much as any of them, but that seemed more trouble than ignoring them.

"Isn't up to her. You and your brother think you're entitled to whatever you want, come in here and take the best piece of ass for miles. I'll tell you—"

Whatever he was about to say was cut off as Dödz's fist connected with his solar plexus, doubling him over. Dödz lifted his arm and brought his elbow down on the back of the man's skull, laying him flat into the mud. Out of his peripheral, Dödz saw the others converging on him, drawing weapons as they moved. He hadn't brought his own weapons out of the tent with him, a mistake he should never have made. But he still wouldn't bet against himself. He leaned back out of the way of the fist coming towards him and jerked to the side, slamming his shoulder into the man's chin and knocking him back. As the man was knocked back, Dödz grabbed the hilt of the sword at his waist and let the man's momentum unsheathe it into his hand.

As soon as the blade was free of the scabbard, Dödz lunged and plunged the blade through the man's chest. Ripping the blade out sideways, he spun the blade around in a tight arc as he turned to face the three others. One had gotten too close, trying to catch him with his back turned, and was caught in the path of the sword. Two of his fingers fell to the ground. The man followed shortly after clutching his bleeding hand and wailing in pain. Dödz kicked him in the face, crushing his nose and knocking loose several teeth, silencing his wailing, before advancing on the last two thugs.

The first, a chubby ginger with a mace, warbled some sort of war cry and charged Dödz. Dödz easily sidestepped the man and kicked the side of his knee. There was a satisfying crunch, and the man toppled, adding his own screams to the chaos of the camp. Dödz considered cutting his throat but figured he wasn't getting back up any time soon. The last man, a trembling youth with a pock-marked face and greasy hair, held his sword at a ready, textbook, like someone who had learned to fight from an instructor but had never sullied his blade on a man.

"You don't want to do this, boy," Dödz growled. The boy shook but held his ground. Dödz walked forward, the sword held loose in his hand. "This is your last warning," he said, but the boy seemed resolute, as if he hadn't just watched Dödz disable his little gang. Maybe he should have slit the ginger's throat. Maybe then this youth would just run the way he should.

"Bringare!" He recognized the Warhawk's voice and cursed under his breath, turning to scan the crowd. There, Adalbert was pushing his way through the throng that had been watching the brief melee, a look of rage on his face. "Godsdamnit, man, what is the meaning of—"

The youth's sword bit into Dödz shoulder, the blow softened by the leather armor but not stopped entirely.

Dödz ducked down, dislodging the blade from his shoulder, and turned as he rose again, ramming his blade into the boy's gut to the hilt. He angled it up so the top of the blade pushed through his stomach, right lung, and out just below the shoulder blade. "I fucking warned you." Dödz spat in the kid's face and shoved him back, releasing the blade. The boy fell, squirming and mewling as he died. There was a deafening silence as Dödz turned back around to face Adalbert, whose face was white as a sheet.

"Damnations, man," he whispered. Then, regaining some of his composure, he turned and shouted, "What are you all staring at! Go about! Clean up this fucking mess!" He turned an angry eye back to Dödz. "And, you, come with me!" He turned on his heel and stormed towards the command tent.

Dödz reached up and clamped a hand over his shoulder to staunch the bleeding, grateful it wasn't his dominant arm. "Godsdamned stupid bullshit," Dödz muttered as he followed the old man. He hadn't needed this. He could have disarmed them all, could have likely ended this without shedding their blood. But that wasn't the Bringare creed. Their father, for all his shittiness, had always taught his brood that when there was a fight, you fought to end it by any means necessary; honor was for the dead. It didn't win them any friends, but it certainly kept them alive.

As Dödz pushed open the tent flap to follow Adalbert, he was greeted by the entire retinue, minus Arik, of course.

"Can someone treat this idiot's wound?" Adalbert snapped.

Anamarie nodded and rushed to get bandages. Dödz sat heavily and starting peeling out of his armor, hissing in pain as the material pulled against his wound.

"What happened to you?" Vaneesa asked.

"The moron started a fight with the Guileclaw boys," Adalbert growled. "So now we're down a squad."

"They jumped me." He shot Vaneesa a significant look.

By the way she turned her head and looked away, it seemed she understood *why* they had jumped him. He had to wonder if it had been part of her plan: protect herself or get one of the annoying brothers murdered, a win-win for her.

"You killed them?" Anamarie asked as she came back and began doing her best to clean him up. "This will sting," she whispered before pouring a bottle of muddy brown spirits over his shoulder. He yelped as the fluid filled his wound with fire but did not complain further as she began wrapping him up.

"Not all of them," Dödz answered as he caught his breath.

"No, but you killed the youngest brother. The survivors of your little escapade are going to demand blood!" Adalbert pointed out.

"And then you can point out that they instigated the fight," Arik said, pushing his way into the tent. "Frankly, Warhawk, you're damn lucky that played out the way it did. Better to lose some unpracticed dirt bags like the Guileclaw gang than a single true warrior. One day, my brother will be woken up with a blade in his gut, but it won't be to idiots like that. No, more likely he'll piss off the wrong noble and end up on the headman's chopping block. Isn't that right, Dödz?"

Dödz smiled at his brother, though it looked a lot more like a snarl than a smile. What did Arik know about his time in Hjortkukstad? Instead of responding to Arik, he turned his face to Anamarie. Without her mask on, he felt like he was meeting her for the first time. She was a swarthy woman, her features broad and flat. He would guess she had grown up near Sarkesh, probably to a family of loggers and lumberjacks. "Thank you," he said as she finished tying the bandage off. She nodded and stepped back. He looked towards Adalbert. "Are you done admonishing me, Herr Warhawk? Can we move on to the plan?"

Adalbert glared daggers at Dödz for a moment before shaking his head and moving to the map sprawled across the table. "While you lot were fetching the final key, another group headed further into the valley and cleared our path towards Kur. Which means we should have a straight march there."

"Assuming they made it, assuming they survived and set up altars," Ward butted in.

"Yes, assuming. They were . . . *are* good men. They won't have abandoned their duty," Adalbert mumbled.

"Your confidence is inspiring, Herr Warhawk," Dödz said, standing.

"So the entire Crusade marches on Kur?" Petyr asked.

"Correct."

"Fantastic. With our might and the might of THEIR blessings, we will crush the undead and grind them beneath our boots, we will end the Bone Heart and free the world of—"

"Save it for the pulpit, Petyr," Arik cut him off. "Let's prepare, then."

# XI

THE MARCH WAS surprisingly uneventful. As promised, the way had largely been cleared by the scouts sent ahead. The column of Crusaders ran across the dismembered corpses of undead, some still twitching, and amongst them, they could spot the smoldering remains of Crusaders who had not been fortunate enough to survive the encounters.

Dödz was glad to see they were burning the bodies. It wouldn't guarantee they would not rise, but it made it less likely, and if they did, a charred body was easier broken than an undamaged one. During the nights, Vaneesa continued to sleep in Dödz's tent. She would slip in just before the last watch would begin and wordlessly lie down. Only Augustus bothered greeting Dödz, jumping onto his shoulder to screech some inane vulgarity before hopping off to search for bugs. He didn't question either the bird or Vaneesa, and no more men accosted him. Perhaps he had taken the fight too far, but it had served his purpose—no one wanted to target him, and now he could exist unharassed for the most part.

On the third day of marching, Arik walked beside Dödz, craning his neck to make sure they were far enough away from the others to not be heard. "So, do you want to tell me what the banshee meant?"

"How the fuck should I know?" Dödz rumbled. He knew his lie wasn't well hidden, that Arik wouldn't let it go with just that.

"Come on, it spoke your name and was talking about someone else too, and then what happened with those liches . . . " Arik pressed.

"Gods," Dödz swore. "Keep your voice down. Do you know how little an excuse any of these Inquisitorial zealots need to kill me? To kill us?" He looked around. "The Misery in Exterg, I have reason to believe this Skelvik was involved. I was waylaid in Hjortkukstad—"

"Yes, I knew that part. You were sentenced to die. I received a letter. It reached me shortly *after* the Misery had taken the whole city."

"Right." Dödz sighed. "Well, I was offered a job to hunt down the local noble's undead wife. It led me to Skelvik. He's been toying with me since, seems to think I'm part of his big prophecy to go against THEM." Dödz shrugged. "I could be wrong. I don't make it my business to figure out what's going through their muddled, rotting brains."

"Unless it's your blade." Arik grinned.

"Exactly." He laughed. It felt odd to laugh with Arik, as though he forgot what a shit-fucker the man was. He quelled his mirth. He needed to remember that given a bag of coins and a whore's promise, Arik would sell him out as quick as look at him. "It's why I'm still here. Whatever Skelvik is or wants, I'm going to kill him, I'm going to end him and, hopefully, make the world just a little less terrible."

"Is it worth it? World's dying anyways," Arik pointed out.

"Maybe. But it's all we got, isn't it?"

Arik nodded and slipped into a thoughtful silence as they continued to march.

Neither brother was a beacon of selfless sacrifice. They had each served in military campaigns that had pulled the wool off their eyes. The world was a dark place, chewing up the naive and spitting out hardened killers and thieves. Good men and woman had all died along with the gods. All that was left were the scum who were too stubborn to die.

But Dödz had always fought harder for a greater good, so long as he was part of the good. Arik, on the other hand, fought for himself. Which begged the question: why was *he* here? What was he doing serving the Warhawk, and what was he getting out of it?

Other brothers might discuss what they had been doing over the years between seeing each other, or maybe they would share fond memories of growing up and talk about other family members, weaving a tapestry of experience and memories to create a quilt of familial understanding and brotherhood. But the Bringare bond of kinship had shattered and lay muddied in the gutters along with the family name. Instead, the two spoke of Skelvik, sharing their knowledge of damned things in order to pinpoint how they could end the creature.

"So we destroy the body, but that's not enough?" Anamarie asked.

Dödz wasn't sure when Anamarie, Vaneesa, Ward, and Petyr had joined the conversation, but as they would likely be heading into battle together, he would rather they know something of what was coming. It made it more likely they would survive. Well, until Ward or Petyr reported them to the church.

"Not if he's a lich," Dödz affirmed.

"*If* he's a lich," Arik said, "we'll need to find where he stores his soul. Only way to destroy them permanently."

"What else could he be? Powerful spell caster, dead—I would think he *has* to be a lich." Ward sniffed.

"Well, there are countless varieties of the damned, Inquisitor," Arik said. "We tend to call magical ones liches, but it could, if we're being honest, be worse. You said he was a saint?"

"Saint Skelvik the—"

"The Pure," Petyr cut in. "I thought you said that name. Saint Skelvik is a great miracle worker in Kergis. You can't mean he has been corrupted."

Arik and Dödz locked eyes. A fallen saint was much worse news than a lich just pretending at sainthood.

"He's not so pure any longer," Dödz finally said.

"That can't be true. I think your definition of purity is skewed. Skelvik is a great man, an incredible saint, someone who—"

"Look!" Ward cut him off, pointing.

Ahead of the column of marching Crusaders, the wall of miasma swirled, and just beyond that, the silhouette of a city could just be made out. There, just inside the miasma, Dödz could make out several scouting groups' worth of broken bodies in torn armor and shattered masks scattered about.

"By SHE, they got torn apart!" Ward exclaimed.

"They've been sacrificed to the Bone Heart," Petyr corrected.

"What?" Ward asked, turning with a horrified look on his face. "Don't say—"

"Petyr, you said Skelvik *is* a great man. You meant *was* a great man, right?" Arik said, a tinge of fear in his voice.

Dödz frowned. He hadn't caught that, but Arik was right. "Petyr." It wasn't a question; it was as much a warning as he could offer as the priest started laughing.

"By Skelvik's graces, you are all so thick!" Petyr cried. Things crawled in the folds of his burnt flesh—scuttling roaches and flies—as the priest seemed to bloat. "He's been speaking to me since you tried to kill me, Dödz. We forgive you. He forgives you."

"Buchardt, what is the meaning of this?" Ward asked, grabbing the priest's shoulder and turning him.

The Inquisitor, never the slow-to-act sort, had already pulled a blade. But Petyr, or rather the thing that had been Petyr Buchardt, lunged forward and bit down into Ward's throat. Dödz rushed forward to grab the priest, to restrain him. Petyr tore back, ripping out flesh and veins from the Inquisitor. Ward's hands came to his throat, trying to staunch the geyser of blood that fountained out of him. He gurgled, unable to articulate with his voice box dangling from Petyr's teeth. He collapsed into the mud, dying quickly, as much a blessing as anything in this age.

Chaos was breaking out everywhere as various Crusaders went mad and began attacking their fellows. Freshly dead monsters who had posed as friends now attacked. The ground shook as monolithic creatures and machines of bone and flesh surged through the miasma towards the column of warriors. They were besieged on all sides.

Dödz wrestled with Petyr, trying to keep his arms behind him, but the priest was happy to dislocate his own shoulders to get out of the hold.

"Arik!" Dödz shouted above the cacophony. "Fucking kill him!"

Arik nodded and rushed forward, drawing a dagger as he did. "I'm sorry, Buchardt," he said as he jammed the blade into the priest's eye. The creature screamed and snapped at Arik but did not die.

"You idiot, you weak fool. Skelvik preserves me, Skelvik empowers me, and the Bone Heart will see you all die!"

Anamarie rushed to the fallen Inquisitor, searching his corpse.

"Hurry!" Dödz cried.

The crusader rushed back, her large armored hands fumbling with a small vial's stopper. *Clever woman*, Dödz thought. The whole time, Petyr was bucking against him, fighting as hard as he could to get free. It took both Bringare brothers to restrain him. Finally getting the stopper free, Anamarie grabbed the priest's face and wrenched his face up toward her. Without preamble or apology, she upended the vial of holy water into the priest's wounded eye socket.

The creature bucked so hard that he threw Dödz and Arik off him with the force of his spasms. He was melting, his flesh running like melted wax, while his rancid blood and bile bubbled up like a frothy ale poured too quickly. His wails ended as his head dissolved, an acrid smoke rising. Still, the body didn't fall. It stood and dissolved, trembling and spasming on its feet, until all that was left was a puddle of noxious innards that fizzed and popped on the ground.

Dödz and the others didn't wait to watch the whole debacle, though. As soon as the creature's head was gone, Arik had ordered that they find the Warhawk. They fought their way through the clutching claws of the undead that surrounded them, each step a war in and of its own. The four of them fought their way through the lines as more and more undead charged into their midst. But finally, they reached Adalbert.

"Warhawk, we can't hold this line forever!" Arik called over the din, dodging the swing of a zombie and swinging his whip out to catch a grotesque out of the air and slam it to the ground.

"We don't have a choice," the old man shouted back. He was dueling with two living shadows. Augustus flew off of Vaneesa's shoulder and harangued the shadows, giving the Warhawk a chance to catch his breath, the bird flitting in and out of reach as its claws dug into the shadow-substance of their flesh. With the bird's help, Adalbert was able to dispatch both creatures—a strange light shone off his blade, and Dödz guessed it was coated in holy oil.

A terrible grinding filled the air, and a thing that looked like a horseless carriage made of iron and bone rolled into view.

"In HIS name, what is that?" Anamarie swore.

"Bone Grinder . . . " Adalbert grunted. "Since we got the final key, they've been active. We need—" He looked haggard. "We need to get in and destroy the heart; it's the only way . . . " He ran to the wagon on the caravan. "Arik, take your squad, get into Kur, find the heart, and destroy it!" He rummaged around, protected by Anamarie as he dropped his guard, until he found a chest. "Here are the keys! I'm counting on you, Arik. Do this, and our agreement is fulfilled. You get what you want."

Dödz heard the words, confirming his suspicions that there was something else going on here, but with the swarm of skeletons marching against them, he didn't have time to confront him now.

Arik grabbed Dödz's arm. "Come, brother. Anamarie, Vaneesa, get your masks on and then with me!" He struggled to get his own mask on.

Dödz did what he could to fend off attacks, protecting Arik as he geared up, trusting his brother would do the same for him. Anamarie and Vaneesa were doing the same dance, covering each other as they got geared up. It reminded Dödz of being in the army, of how small groups *could* work together. He fastened his own mask on while Arik protected him, then the four warriors broke off from the column, fighting every inch of the way to the gates of Kur.

XII

THE FIGHTING TO get to Kur was terrible. The four of them arrived at the gates bloody and worn down but knowing the worst was ahead of them. The city of Kur was a massive, spiraling pit into the ground, homes and businesses built into the concentric cliffs going down into the earth. The dead stalked through the city as if they were living. Going about their unlives the same as one would see in any city in the dying lands. The only real difference was the stench of humanity—the stink of sweat and sour excrement that marked mankind's presence—was replaced by the cloying scent of decay and rot. It was also quieter. There was a terrible, keening screaming emanating from all around them, but the normal bustle and drama of a living city was oddly absent. Around the pit and city, a great wall and gate had been constructed from the bones of some nightmarish monster. Dödz couldn't identify what sort of beast it had been, wouldn't even know where to begin how to identify the alien bones that made up the construction of Kur.

But the oddest thing was that they were no longer being attacked. As soon as they had reached the gates, it was as if they were children who had reached *base* during tag. In the distance, they could still hear the pitched battle of the Crusaders fighting off the valley's dead. But the four of them stood unmolested at the threshold of a near mythical city.

"What is that terrible sound?" Anamarie asked.

"Soul ingots," Vaneesa answered. "They smelt souls and bones in furnaces and create iron from it, cursed metal that screams its anguish." She sounded solemn, and Dödz made a note to ask her how she knew this after they finished their task, assuming they survived.

Dödz walked through the gates, every muscle in his body tensed, waiting for the dead to stop what they were doing and attack. But the attack never came. A few Kur citizens stopped and stared, some pointed, and it was obvious they were talking among themselves. But it was the behavior of small-town folk seeing strangers in their midst, not that of some horrible mastermind. The living had come to the city of the dead, and they were no more a threat than any tourist in any other city. Dödz kept moving.

"Dödz!" Arik jogged to catch up. "Where are you going? We need to figure out where the Bone Heart is."

Dödz stopped and looked at his brother, glad that the mask was hiding his contempt. "Really? You want to ask directions? You want to piece together the mystery?" He paused as Vaneesa and Anamarie joined them. "My brother thinks we need to waste time investigating the city and interviewing its people so we can find our target. Or maybe, hear me out, Arik, we can go down the fucking pit in the center of the city that the miasma is pouring out of. Do you think maybe the heart is down there, or are you hoping for a literal wooden sign pointing the way?"

"Fuck you, Dödz, you are not in charge of this squad," Arik growled.

"No, and neither are you," Anamarie pointed out. "I am, and I think Dödz has a point. We make our way down the pit. Quickly. The entire Bone Heart Crusade is counting on us." She turned and started jogging towards the center of town, looking for ways to descend into the pit.

Dödz and Vaneesa joined her, forcing Arik to run to catch up once he got over himself.

It was a surreal experience. Dödz had faced off against hordes of the undead, and he had been close to the creatures without fighting them, but those times were few and far between. This entire city of the dead felt like he had slipped through a portal to a different reality.

They travelled through the city at a good pace, no more than whispered gossip dogging their descent down the pit. The screaming had faded into low, annoying background noise, and Dödz was amazed to see so much mundanity in his surroundings. If you removed the choking miasma and clothed these figures in flesh, it could be any city in these dying lands.

"Uncanny, isn't it?" Arik asked, watching a skeletal woman in a bonnet scrubbing clothes in a wash basin while, next door to her, a rotting butcher prepared some sort of rancid meat for customers who hadn't needed to eat in years.

"Unsettling," Dödz responded, and then pointed. "Look there, that must be it."

They had reached the bottom of the pit, a wide, flat area littered with unmoving skeletal remains. Ahead of them, in the side of the pit, was a massive iron door that screamed into the miasma-choked day. A relief was carved upon the doors of a massive heart with four keyholes dug into it, one for each chamber. The door could only lead one place.

"Let's go." Dödz rushed forward but was brought up short as the entire pit began to tremble. All around them, blue ectoplasmic mist rose from the ground. The bones they had been walking on shook and rose into the air, forming half spectral, half-skeletal warriors that brandished ethereal weapons at them. "Fuck."

Arik's whip cracked past Dödz, crushing the forming ribcage of a warrior and causing the blue mist to dissipate. "Fuck them, you mean," Arik snarled before starting to race towards the door. "Let's go!"

"Getting real tired of this shit," Dödz growled, following suit.

All around them, the monsters were forming and

coming forward. There were humanoid shapes, but undead rising from the ground was unlimited in its variety. Arik was a flurry, a maelstrom of leather and steel, creating a barrier of crackling holy energy with his whip that kept the creatures at bay. Vaneesa was a lithe blur, her daggers striking out at anything that got close enough to prove a threat. Of course, her blades did nothing to the ghostly apparitions—they had no flesh to tear, no blood to spill—but she was moving quickly enough to at least not get hurt.

Anamarie was a titan, a juggernaut of steel. She struck with the flat of her great sword, powdering bone as she moved. Dödz was glad she was on his side, though the flash of memory from fighting Numen worried him. As they moved, the attacks were getting worse, an army of ghosts and skeletal amalgamations coming for them. The thunderous roar of ghostly hooves filled the air. A skeletal lancer riding a spectral horse charged at them from the east. Anamarie saw them coming, her mask turning towards this new threat.

She angled her body away from the charge and slammed her sword into the earth, deflecting the lance, then her body twisted and she slammed her armored fist into the horse's head, right between its rolling white eyes. The spirit beast crashed to the ground, skidding past them and dragging its rider along with it. Arik's whip struck out, ripping the skeletal rider's skull off its body and flinging it across the pit.

Dödz was tempted to stop and admire the sheer strength and brutality of his companion but knew that to stop moving was to die. The short distance across the pit, no more than forty meters or so, had felt like kilometers of ground to cover. But they had reached the door. Arik began franticly looking for a way to open it while Vaneesa and Anamarie protected him.

"Get that door open, godsdamnit!" Dödz roared.

"Trying!" Arik shouted back. A moment later, he laughed as he found a recess in the wall and dug his fingers in.

Dödz followed his example on the other side of the door and pulled with all of his might. Slowly but surely, the doors peeled back, spilling copious amount of the toxic miasma out, creating a dense, nearly impenetrable wall of fog all around them.

"Let's go!" Dödz shouted.

"No," Anamarie growled as she slammed her blade against the head of a massive bone serpent. "Vaneesa and I will hold them back!"

"What?" Vaneesa screeched.

"We have to give them a chance to destroy the heart!"

Vaneesa looked like she was going to argue, but then she nodded and darted into the fog, off to cause chaos and slow the onslaught.

"Go!" Anamarie roared as she stationed herself before the opening of the door, spinning her massive blade above her head to bring it down on a schlorping mess of a grotesque that got too close.

Dödz didn't like it. Anamarie was a beast of a woman, but how long could she truly survive out here before she was overwhelmed? And as fast as Vaneesa was, how long before her stamina gave out? The dead had no limitations; they would keep coming past the point where she collapsed and would then devour her body and soul. But staying up here would only mean that he would be with them when they fell, that his body would be added to the casualties and the enemies in turns. No, the only hope they had was to get to the heart and end this once and for all.

He turned his head to shout to Arik to come with him, only to discover his brother was already disappearing into the darkness of the doorway. The man had no qualms about letting others die in his place. Maybe it was why he looked so much younger, so much more carefree than Dödz. It didn't matter. What needed to be done needed to be done. He followed Arik into the miasmic abyss.

XIII

IT WAS SURPRISINGLY well lit down in the catacombs under Kur. Dödz had thought to light his lantern, but as soon as the light from the doorway—as dim as it was—faded, it was replaced by veins of glowing ore that carved through the tunnel like the track marks in the arm of an addict, radiating a bruised light that was suffused by the miasma. Everything pulsed with the rapid thumping coming from somewhere ahead of him. Dödz recognized the sound; it was a heartbeat in panic.

"Arik!" Dödz called, his voice echoing through the tunnel.

No answer.

"Damnit, Arik!" he called again, picking up speed to run forward.

He was worried he could trip over something, about some terror hiding in the mist waiting to rear up and disembowel him, but these were fears he had no power over, things that would either happen or not. All he could do was press forward. He carried his lantern shield in front of his body, hoping that if an attack did come, it would do so at chest height and be deflected.

Suddenly, the miasma thinned and was illuminated before him. Torches lit at regular intervals sputtered to life with vile blue flames vomiting thick, greasy smoke into the air.

"I told you he would come." The voice was cruel and raspy, like a blade sliding across dried velum. Dödz recognized it immediately.

"Skelvik," he hissed.

The mist swirled around Dödz as it parted, revealing a massive cavern. At its center stood the dread bishop Skelvik in all of his undead glory and rotting finery. Next to him, a gargantuan heart, like the muscle of some unknown titan that beat in a frantic frenzy. It was attached to the ceiling and the floor of the cavern through blackened veins as thick as Dödz's legs, and with each beat, it pumped more miasma into the air. Across its thick, muscular chambers, thick, bony plates protected its flesh.

But the heart was not what commanded his attention; instead, he was fixated on Arik, who stood beside Skelvik. His gasmask had been removed, and he swayed slowly from side to side, his eyes and expression vacant.

"Arik . . . what are you doing?"

"Oh, don't worry, he lives. And I know your thoughts, Bringare. You think he has betrayed you yet again, don't you?" Skelvik's rictus grin widened as he watched Dödz's eyes narrow. "Yes, you do. But no, not this time. Though I suppose it was only a matter of time. He wants to betray you. He hates you. Almost as much as you hate him. All that I need, all that anyone needs, Dödz, is a little push." Skelvik stepped back and nodded.

Arik's head snapped up, his eyes locking with Dödz's. "You upstart little freak!" He snarled and walked forward, drawing a knife from his belt as he moved.

"Snap out of it, Arik. You don't want to do this. You're here to end the heart, just the same as me!" Dödz growled.

"Oh, I'll destroy it, of course I will. I'll destroy it and be rewarded, but my poor little brother, poor Dödz didn't make it. No more brother outshining me, no more brother to steal all of mother's affection, no more little fucking brother with his somber droll eyes to woo the women who are meant for me!" He smiled cruelly. "You never could just leave well enough alone. Your practiced indifference and haughty ego are a poison to this world, Dödz, and I will cure it."

Dödz raised his shield. "This isn't you, Arik. Skelvik is in your head."

"And what if he is . . . Dödz? Is anything I'm saying untrue? Go on, lie more, as you always do."

Dödz said nothing. There was no sense in it. Arik wouldn't be able to care that he was as great a liar as any Bringare, or that Arik had in fact done his fair share of swooping in to woo women with his easy charm and confidence. He wouldn't care about any of that. He was incapable of reason so long as Skelvik was in his skull.

Arik paused in his advance. "He's right, you know. You're going to be the end of everything, but I can stop it. I can stop you. Your death saves me, Dödz, and it is a burden I will happily carry." He charged.

Arik's dagger flashed out, going straight for his throat. Dödz raised the blade affixed to his gauntlet to deflect it, but the attack had been a feint, and Arik's boot came up and kicked Dödz in the stomach, pushing him back. Dödz ducked under the next punch and launched an uppercut into Arik's solar plexus. He doubled over, and Dödz brought his knee up to catch him on the right cheek, throwing him back.

Arik rose, cradling his head with one hand, but struck out with a reverse grip that caught Dödz's mask and ripped it painfully off his head, tearing hair out as it came off. The choking miasma filled Dödz's lungs, and he coughed, barely catching Arik's blade as it came in with his buckler.

His entire body was on fire, and his eyes watered. It was all he could do to deflect two more strikes as Arik pressed the advantage. Dödz ducked under the next strike and kicked out, sweeping Arik's leg out from under him. Arik landed with a thud on his back.

Dödz dove forward, grappling for Arik's arm. He grabbed his wrist and slammed it against the ground, using his other arm to block blows from Arik's free hand. After three blows, the dagger skittered across the stone with a clatter.

Arik rolled to his chest and pushed off the ground, jerking forward to wrap his arms around Dödz's stomach in a tackle. Dödz brought his elbow down on Arik's shoulder as the man tried to squeeze the oxygen out of him. Arik surged up and slammed his forehead into Dödz's nose. The sound of crackling cartilage echoed in his skull, and his nostrils filled with blood as his nose crumpled against Arik's skull. Dödz stumbled back as he reached up, pressed his nose between both hands, and wrenched it to the front, resetting it as best as he could.

Through the pain-haze, he saw Arik scrambling for the blade. He rushed forward and kicked Arik in the ribs with a satisfying crunch, sending him rolling to the side. Arik clutched his side as he rolled, and Dödz took the opportunity to kick the dagger far out of reach.

Dödz turned his back on his brother and made a run towards Skelvik. If he could kill the creature, it should break its hold on Arik. He made it ten steps before the crack of Arik's whip filled the cavern.

The leather and metal length of the whip wrapped around Dödz's ankle. A half-breath later, Arik yanked the whip, ripping Dödz off his feet. He twisted as he fell and landed on his back, kicking his leg to try to free his foot from the whip. Arik pulled the whip back, the whip ripping against Dödz's flesh as it recoiled. Dödz threw his legs up and then used the momentum to flip back to his feet, bringing his shield up in the same movement on instinct.

The whip slammed into his shield, sending painful shocks throughout his arm and shoulder. Dödz charged forward, but the whip was faster. The metal tip smashed into his right shoulder, forcing Dödz to drop the shield as his arm hung limply at his side.

Arik struck again, but Dödz raised his still-functioning arm, lunging so that the weapon wrapped around his forearm. He yanked back hard, causing Arik to stumble forward, and at the moment he reached his brother, he leapt up and lashed out with both legs, connecting in a terrible kick against Arik's chest. He felt the rippling of cracking bones under his feet before he fell to the ground. The impact tore a scream from his lips, but he rolled onto his chest and pushed himself to standing as quickly as he could.

Arik was still writhing on the ground, the pain too much for him to rise. Dödz stumbled to him and straddled his chest, bringing a strangled cry of pain from Arik as he put pressure on Arik's bruised and cracked ribs. Dödz ignored his cries and brought down his left fist in a punch. He rained down blows until Arik stopped moving, his eyes swollen shut. He was still breathing, the bubbles of blood along his lips evidence of that.

Dödz rose, pulling himself off his brother, and turned towards Skelvik and the heart. It still beat franticly, as though it knew the end was near. He could feel the shards of bone like broken glass in his shoulder filling him with a screaming agony. He ignored it, his full attention on the undead madman who continuously brought pain to his life.

"And what will you do now, Bringare? Fratricide aside, you have no means to destroy the heart. You come to me once again powerless and weak." Skelvik's voice, as dry and dead as it was, was full of mirth.

Dödz smiled. "I'm going to do what Arik promised to do and destroy that fucking heart."

"Oh, you and what magical relic? What god ordained you a champion that you can bring holy judgment down on the Bone Heart of the Valley?" Skelvik asked, floating higher in the cavern and flitting about while mocking Dödz.

Dödz didn't answer. He walked forward, closing the distance between himself and the heart. When he was only five feet away, he let the whip, Arik's whip with the holy teste of Saint Barthakus of Grift in its tip, unfurl to the ground.

"Oh . . . " Skelvik said, his voice dripping with contemptuous hate.

Dödz lifted his arm and, with a flick of his wrist, lashed out with the weapon. He was not as practiced as Arik with a whip, but he knew how to wield one effectively enough. The length of leather and wire shot forward and cracked against the bone armor of the heart, but the armor was useless. The whip broke through the bone plate effortlessly and tore into the heart. The thing's beating slowed, each haggard thump taking longer to labor through.

"Ah, you can always be counted on, Dödz Bringare, to do the right thing, to answer the call, to serve fate. I would stay and kill you, but I have pressing matters in the Svmp." Skelvik's laugh roared through the cavern, near deafening.

"You're going nowhere, monster!" Dödz brought the whip back, intent on shutting the lich up for good, when the Bone Heart exploded. It sent miasma, bone fragments, and blackened leather flesh everywhere. The force of the blast threw Dödz back, and he rolled across the ground for several meters, blissfully unconscious.

XIV

DÖDZ WOKE IN his tent. The world was blurry and painfully bright, despite the sky outside the tent being its normal colorless gray. "Gods . . . "

"Good morning, Dödz," Arik said from a nearby chair.

"Arik . . . you're alive." He was surprised to find that he was relieved to see it.

"Despite your best efforts, brother." Arik chuckled and then shook his head. His face was a mass of swollen bruises. "And thanks to the trials of Anamarie and Vaneesa."

"What happened?" Dödz asked.

"Well, whatever you did after you beat the shit out of me—"

"You were going to kill me."

"I'm not blaming you. Not this time." Arik sighed and stood, stretching. "The miasma stopped pouring out. Anamarie says that every citizen of Kur threw down their arms and wailed, like the whole city was defeated. I'm guessing that's when you destroyed the heart. They came down and found us both . . . in the shape they found us in and dragged us back out of the city. I'm guessing Anamarie did most of that. But apparently, the entire valley felt the heart's demise, because the attacks on the crusade line died off too."

"So we're just outside of Kur? How long have I been out?"

"Days. We're actually in the final camp. I woke up a few hours later. Head feels like scrambled egg, but . . . whole . . . "

"Days." Dödz hissed, struggling to rise. His ribs ached, but his shoulder, his shoulder was on fire.

"Careful, you're still healing, and besides, the Warhawk—"

"Can speak for himself," Adalbert said, pushing aside the tent flap and approaching the siblings. "I told you to come get me when he woke up," he growled.

"He just woke. I was filling him in before I came to get you, that's all," Arik grumbled and stepped back.

"Glad to see you recovering, Bringare," Adalbert said.

"Glad to be recovering. I suppose this is where you tell me to get the hell out of your camp?" Dödz asked.

"Well, honestly, I would prefer if your brother, you, and, and the others stayed with the Crusade. We may have accomplished our mission here, but the end of the world is ever approaching, and we don't know what evils may arise." He let the statement hang in the air. If he hoped Dödz would take the bait, he was to be disappointed.

"I have my own evils to hunt and my own life to live, however little of it is left," Dödz said finally.

"Yes, I'm sure that's true. Well, in that case, I'll make good on my promise, assuming that your request is the same as your brother's." He tossed an envelope onto Dödz's chests. "A full pardon for your crimes, known and unknown, in the eyes of the Church and in the territories of Galgenbeck."

Dödz stared down at the envelope and then shot a look at Arik. So that was what this was, keeping his own head out of the hangman's noose. A desperate ploy to avoid repercussions for his own actions. Dödz considered stating that he was currently not wanted for any crimes that he knew of. But then he considered the Inquisitors he had murdered outside of Postek and thought better of it. "Thank you," he said numbly.

"A payment of twenty-five silver." Adalbert dropped the bag of coins next to Dödz's sleeping bag. "And . . . because your brother sued for it, you may keep the tent for your personal travels and use." He looked between the two and shook his head. "You're sure I cannot convince either of you to join our ranks permanently?"

"No, Warhawk. I've fought for armies before; I don't intend to die doing so now," Dödz said.

"And I can think of better ways to spend the remainder of the world," Arik added. "But thank you. If our paths cross again, it won't be as enemies but allies." He offered the Warhawk his hand.

The two men shook, and Adalbert departed.

"A pardon?" Dödz asked.

"I was arrested outside the Temple of the Two in Galgenbeck," Arik admitted. "Not my fault they train such comely priestesses."

"You're disgusting." Dödz chuckled.

"At least we agree on that," Vaneesa said, pushing her way into the tent, followed by Anamarie. Augustus immediately took flight from her shoulder and landed on Dödz. The bird preened and marched back and forth across his stomach before shouting "Dog-licker!" and nuzzling his face.

"I missed you too, Augustus." Dödz looked up at the women. "My brother says I owe you both my life. Thank you."

"I wasn't about to leave you behind." Anamarie smiled. She had an easy and honest smile. "Not after the great things you two have done."

"And Augustus would have been annoyed had his favorite verbal punching bag gone missing," Vaneesa added.

Dödz nodded. "Fair enough. What will you two do now? Carry on with Adalbert and the Crusades?"

Anamarie shot Arik a look and sighed. "You did not tell him?"

"He just woke up!" Arik cried, exasperated. "Just a moment ago. I've not had a moment to tell him shit without being interrupted."

"Tell me what, Anamarie?" Dödz asked, waving Arik off.

"We're coming with you," she said plainly.

"Coming with me? What does that mean?" he asked.

"You're going to hunt him, Skelvik the Profane. Right?" Arik asked.

"Yes, but why does that matter to you?" he asked.

"Skelvik took over Petyr, corrupted him. He was . . . he was my cousin," Anamarie said sadly. "But more than that, the creature is pure evil, intent on bringing on the Miseries. I can't sit back and let him roam this world when I can act." She looked resolute, and Dödz couldn't blame her.

"And you? Why do you care?" he asked his brother.

Arik shrugged. "That beast was in my brain, Dödz. He crawled in my soul and played me like a puppet. I could tell you I want the world to be better, that I want to aid my brother. But at the end of it, I want to see the thing destroyed. I feel like there is a stain on my very being from his presence that only his erasure will cleanse."

Dödz couldn't argue with that. He felt the same disgusting corruption, the same feeling that until Skelvik's skull lay shattered and lifeless on the ground before him, he could never be whole again. He raised an eyebrow to Vaneesa. "I would think you would be glad to be done with the Bringare brothers."

"You wouldn't be wrong, but I've served my time with the Crusade. I don't like directionless wars against concepts. They want to fight evil in all its forms, good for them, but the whole Crusade will be nothing more than another army for Josilfa, and I'm not interested in being a pawn in that particular struggle."

"Any idea where to start?" Arik asked when Dödz didn't offer any argument.

"Unfortunately, yes. It's not a place I look forward to going to again, but if we want to track Skelvik, it's the only lead we have," Dödz said while studiously avoiding eye contact.

"Well, don't leave us hanging, man! Where are we going?" Anamarie asked.

"North, to Sarkash . . . to the Svmp deep within its boundaries."

EPILOGUE

THEY HAD TRAVELED together, the four of them, nonstop until they reached the edge of the valley leading into the Wästland. There, Arik finally demanded that they rest. They unloaded their gear and set up their tents, a nice little parting gift from the Crusade. A small fire used to cook some unidentifiable animal that Vaneesa had caught, and then they each went to their own tent.

Dödz was just getting comfortable on his bedroll when he heard the rustling of the tent flap. He heard a gentle squawking and flutter of wings, and then the light footfalls of Vaneesa, a sound he had grown used to during his time with the Crusades.

"What are you doing here? Is Arik bothering you?" he asked without turning over to look at her. She didn't respond, but he heard her dropping something to the ground—her bedroll, he assumed. A moment later, he felt her lift the edge of his threadbare blanket and slip under it beside him. He froze, almost holding his breath. "What are you do—"

"Shut up, Bringare," she whispered into his ear, her naked body pressing against his back. "Don't embarrass me by rejecting me. Do not shame me by making me spell it out."

He rolled in the bedroll to face her. He considered her face in the darkness of the tent. He had avoided growing close to anyone for years, since the sky had gone gray. But here in the dark, he couldn't deny her.

He pushed forward, meeting her lips in a desperate kiss, the pent-up need for connection breaking forth for both of them. She returned the kiss, biting his lip and forcing her tongue in his mouth as she reached down to undo his belt and get him out of his pants. They moved together in the darkness, no thoughts or doubts invading their minds until they were spent and could move no more.

Dödz lay back, relishing the weight of Vaneesa on his chest, one of her legs draped over his waist. Her fingers traced the patterns of his scars across his chest, and slowly, under her sweet administrations, he fell asleep.

His dreams were of violence, the undead rising all around and reaching for him with rotting, diseased claws. Each direction he turned, he was surrounded by a wall of the angry dead, each bearing the face of some loved one or ally he had left behind in a shallow grave somewhere along life. He fought tooth and nail, but there were just so many. They swiftly overwhelmed him and dragged him forward against his will.

There was a sudden break in the wall of dead, and he was treated to a black sun above a blood-drenched earth, the vista of a once grand city torn apart. A centipede that towered over the world crushed buildings and chapels under its countless legs. It turned its terrifying gaze to Dödz and spread its mandibles to shriek . . .

"COCKSUCKER!"

Dödz awoke with a start to Augustus standing on his chest, shouting.

"Ugh, Augustus . . . thank you," he grumbled.

"Dödz!" Arik called from outside the tent.

"What?" he called back, looking around the tent for Vaneesa. She was nowhere to be seen, but there on top of his gear was a carefully folded note. He frowned as he saw it, staring at it as he pulled on his trousers. He grabbed the note and shoved it in his pocket. He would read it later, but he was sure he already knew what it said. *"Thanks for the night, keep my bird safe, fuck you Bringare, hugs and kisses, Vaneesa."* Try as he might, he couldn't be angry. Though he did wonder why she left the bird.

"Dödz!" Arik called again, sounding more frantic.

Dödz grabbed his hand axe from the ground and came out of the tent. "What, damnit?" he asked before he saw a scout from the Crusades standing there. The man looked ragged and despondent. "What?" Dödz asked again more gently.

"Lords, I . . . I am sorry, the Warhawk is dead."

"Dead?" Dödz asked. "What the fuck do you mean? He was in perfect health when we left . . . " He shot a look at Arik.

"Most assuredly, lord, but yesternight, as the twilight was descending, there was a terrible sound, like all of the gods screaming at once, and a swarm . . . "

"A swarm?" Arik asked.

"A swarm of insects blackened the sky. They came from the direction of Kur, and they burned with a blue hateful light. Wasps, bees, roaches, flies, all manner of biting insects, my lords. They descended upon the camp and . . . they ate . . . lords . . . they devoured all the living flesh . . . I saw the Warhawk . . . They filled his mouth and eyes, lords. They ate him from within."

"How did you escape, then?"

"Oh, lords . . . " The man began weeping. "I did not . . . I was stung many times during my flight. I can feel them in me, breeding, filling me . . . " As he spoke, maggots began pouring from his mouth, things with too many legs scrambling from between his eyelids, trying to get free.

Dödz shouted and darted to the fire, grabbed an unlit lantern, and threw it with all his might at the messenger, where it burst, dousing the man in oil. Arik, quick on the uptake, grabbed a still smoldering stick from the fireplace and stabbed into the man, who quickly lit up with a horrible scream. The air was filled with the stench of burning hair, flesh, and insects. Anamarie ran out of her tent just in time to watch the man, a charred husk still screaming in agony, collapse onto the ground and die.

Dödz stared down at the man and then stared off the way they had come. The sky was dark, writhing with untold number of insects buzzing in the distance.

"Gods," Arik whispered.

"Not for many years," Dödz answered. "Let's get moving. We have a saint to murder."

2:1 As at the beginning, so at the end, all manner of fly and wasp shall fill the air.
2:2 and the ground pale with maggots.

Lair of the Bone Fiend

A One-Shot by Kevin Welch

In a tavern not unlike the dozen you've seen in half as many days, you and your "party" sit and watch Dödz drink away his past transgressions in complete silence. As you spend your miniscule per diem on ale and other vices, you overhear some inebriated locals speculate about missing livestock, drug away in the cover (of night?). Inquiring with the locals doesn't bring much more information other than it's been happening for weeks and—aside from the drag marks—the only other clues are smaller than normal footprints.

Seeing Dödz has had his fill for the night and retired to his room, you and the party decide to look into this… Who knows, there may be some extra silver in it for you all …

Following the drag marks leads the party to an abandoned shack a couple miles out of town. Entering shows a long stairway leading into an unlit chamber. There are two open doors to either side and a long hallway leading further into darkness. For as dark as the chamber is, a lot of noise echoes throughout. The whole place stinks of stale smoke, rotten flesh, and thick blood.

LAIR OF THE BONE FIEND
2
1
3
5
4
KW '25
5 FT

Room 1

The room is littered with crates and random supplies.
Passing a Dr12 presence test and a d4 roll will
reveal:
(Roll from core book)

  1) Weapons
  2) Armor
  3) Corpse Plundering
  4) Starting Equipment

On the south wall is a barred door leading to a dark
hall. Dr14 presence test or the false floor trap is
triggered, with a 30 ft drop onto jagged spikes. No
save! Instant death!

Room 2

Shuffling of feet echoes from this room. Entering
reveals d6+1 Gnome-sized lackeys, bloodletting the
abducted livestock and cutting flesh from bone.
Entering catches them off guard.

GNOMISH LACKEY
Short, blood-drenched, angry
HP - 4 Armor - bloody tunic -d2

Room 3

Down the dark set of stairs is a room filled with rotten meat and entrails being ground up into paste by d2+1 primate amalgamations, stitched together with whatever spare parts are around.

PATCHWORK PRIMATE
Large, hostile, rotten flesh
HP - 10 Armor - Thick hide -d4
Punch attack - d6 dmg, dr12 toughness test or stunned.

If the PC is stunned, Patchwork Primate will attempt to grind the PC in a meat grinder. Dr12 presence to break stun condition or they're ground up for d4 rounds.

Down the hall from room 3 is an alcove with a pit full of blood.

Room 4

Open room, full of bones, smells of sweet rot.
Large pile of bones in the center of the room. Dr12 presence test shows the bones shift slightly. Entering the room triggers the bones to form into a large skeletal creature, grinding and clattering towards the players.

BAGGO BONES
Splintered, jagged, foul
HP - 8 Armor - None
Thrown Bone Attack - d6 dmg, dr12 agility to dodge.

Reassemble - when brought to 0 HP for the first time, bones will reassemble in d4 rounds and stalk party.

Room 5

Locked door, dr12 agility to pick lock.

Opening the door reveals a figure hunched over the corpse of a desiccated bovine, blood long drained from the body. The figure arises and resembles the "man" Dödz told a story of long ago… using the term man very loosely… More of a bag of flesh occupied by roughly 351 rodent-sized flies. A man everyone thought long dead. This is your livestock thief… a "man" known as Rundle Mykrawpinoose.

RUNDLE MYKRAWPINOOSE
HP - 10 Armor - Loose fitting skin -d2

LORD OF FLIES
Once per combat the flies that compose Rundle's body can be used as a ranged attack. Damage 1d6 with 1 in 6 chance that the injured enemy by this attack dies because of an infection in 10 minutes.

FLESH AND BONE
When Rundle is down to half HP, the flies that comprise his body will inhabit the bovine corpse he was feasting on, adding 8 HP and another -d2 armor.

Conclusion

Arriving back to town with what you've discovered falls on deaf ears. "A man made of flies? Tiny gnome-like men? What do you take us for?! Idiots?? Get out of town or we will string ya up!"

Lord of Flies Class by Eduardo Carabaño
Adventure inspiration from Flail to the Face Episode 12: To Schleswig! Part Two: Ulterior Motives (with John Baltisberger)

Something Shambles Forth

An Undead Generator

The stink of rot fills your nostrils. A chill fills the air and stitches itself to your bones. The dead are coming, and they are hungry.

What Did It Used to Be? (d20)

1. Human (Adult) HP 6
2. Dog HP 5
3. Stag HP 10
4. Bull HP 15
5. Giant Spider HP 16
6. Locust Swarm HP 12
7. Tiger HP 17
8. Goblin HP 4
9. Horse HP 11
10. Flock of Birds HP 16
11. Bear HP 18
12. Troll HP 29
13. Pig HP 8
14. Cow HP 11
15. Snake HP 5
16. Human (Child) HP 2
17. Elephant HP 20
18. Giant HP 36
19. Wyrm HP 31
20. God HP 78

What Raised It? (d6)

1. Demons
2. Virus
3. Necromancy
4. Vengeful Gods
5. Curse
6. Dumb fucking luck

How Many? (d20)

1-4. 1
5-8. d2
9-12. d3
13-16. d4
17-20. d6

Does It Have Armor? (d4)

1. No
2. Tattered Clothes or Flesh, Soft Form: -d2
3. Thick or Chitinous Hide: -d4
4. Strangely Pristine Plate Mail: -d6

How Much Damage Does It Do? (d20)

      1-4. d2
      5-8. d4
     9-12. d6
    13-16. d8
    17-20. d10

How Do You Sense Its Presence? (d20)

     1-2. That awful smell
     3-4. Pained moans on the wind
     5-6. A distant shuffling
     7-8. A chill that cuts to your core
    9-10. A thickening trail of blood and organs
    11-12. Survivors running for their lives
    13-14. Lost and bloodied children
    15-16. Signs reading "Beware the Dead!"
    17-18. An old man with no eyes and a tale to tell
    19-20. No warning. You're fucked!

What Can Kill It? (d20)

1. Steel	11. Blooded Iron
2. Fire	12. Removing Its Tongue
3. Magic	13. Baptism
4. Cold	14. Sacrifice
5. Holy Water	15. A Sacred Vow
6. Wood	16. Silver
7. Forgiveness	17. Electricity
8. Prayer	18. Decapitation
9. Sacrilegious Rites	19. Dismemberment
10. Tears	20. Ohmygoditwon'tstaydown!

ABOUT THE AUTHOR

John Baltisberger is a multi-award winning author and game designer of speculative and genre fiction and gonzo games. Known for his brutal splatterpunk, occult musings, and innovative prose, John has written sci-fi, fantasy, horror, poetry, nonfiction, and romance. When not writing fiction, John edits, writes, and designs games like the Wandie-winning Odd Gobs and the Ennie-winning Obscure. He is well known for his work in the Mork Borg space for having written several novelizations of the game and for creating third-party content such as Morkkabeans and Apostles of Affliction.

Beyond his writing career, John is the Publishing Editor of Madness Heart Press, including its imprints; Aggadah Try It and Gutter Mystic Books, which focuses on transgressive fiction, Jewish genre fiction, and gonzo nonfiction respectively. He is also the Creative Director of Madness Heart Games, which focuses on creating interesting TTRPGS and pioneering the BADASS system. He can be found at http://linktr.ee/kaijupoet.

MORE FROM JOHN BALTISBERGER

Abhorrent Siren
Abhorrent Accords
Blood & Mud
All I Want is to Take Shrooms & Listen to the Color of Nazi Screams
Unclean Verses
Whispers of the Dead Saint
War of Dictates
Jungles of Habbiel
Children of the Gods
No Guilt of Bloodshed
The Hillels Have Eyes
Treif Magic
Son of the Righ Hand
Sheyd of Gray